I0535112

BLOOD AND JEWELS

THE CASKET GIRLS

FAMILY 1

A.D. BRAZEAU

The characters and events in this book are fictitious. Any similarity to real persons, living or dead, places, or events is coincidental and not intended by the author.

If you purchase this book without a cover you should be aware that this book may have been stolen property and reported as "unsold and destroyed" to the publisher. In such case the author has not received any payment for this "stripped book."

Blood and Jewels
The Casket Girls Family: 1
Copyright © 2025 AD Brazeau
All rights reserved.

ISBN: (ebook)
(print)

Inkspell Publishing
207 Moonglow Circle #101
Murrells Inlet, SC 29576

Edited By Yezanira Venecia
Cover art By Emily's World By Design

All Rights Reserved. No part of this book may be used, including but not limited to, the training of or use by artificial intelligence, or reproduced in any manner whatsoever without written permission, except in the case of brief quotations embodied in critical articles and reviews. This book, or parts thereof, may not be reproduced in any form without permission. The copying, scanning, uploading, and distribution of this book via the internet or via any other means without the permission of the publisher is illegal and punishable by law. Please purchase only authorized electronic or print editions, and do not participate in or encourage piracy of copyrighted materials. Your support of the author's rights is appreciated.

DEDICATION

For those still on the journey of self-discovery

AD BRAZEAU

CHAPTER ONE

Khaos thanked the gods he wasn't human.

A regular human male, fragile and prone to things like heart attacks and liver disease, would never have been able to survive the night he'd just had. But for Khaos, a high-born demon, there wasn't enough alcohol on the planet to kill him. He reaped all the benefits, had all the fun, and then woke up fresh as a daisy in the morning.

Khaos opened his eyes as a morning sunbeam warmed one giant foot hanging half off the couch. He stretched his arms briefly before registering the petite body tucked alongside him. He froze, naked as a jaybird. The young lady was curled on her side, her long black hair half across her face, one leg thrown over his thigh, a soft snore issuing every time she took a breath.

If he didn't think fast, this wouldn't end well. Especially when his mother had returned from the Underworld only the day before. Bringing women home wasn't looked upon favorably. At first, this behavior had been tolerated, but the more random humans he'd brought into the house, the more his parents had frowned upon his activities. His mother had once uttered the words *Enough is enough.*

He would have to think fast to get the current woman out of there without his mother, Greer, catching wise. Khaos gently took hold of the nameless woman's leg and moved it to the couch while he wormed to the edge. Once on his feet, he scoured the room for his clothes, cursing his stupidity.

Not only had he brought a woman home, but they'd made good use of the formal living room. A chair was turned over. The leg of a side table was broken, the table leaning against the wall for support, and a lamp, no doubt as expensive as it was old, lay in a shattered heap below the broken table. It was a good thing the room was hardly used. No one ever sat there because the room was on the bottom floor of the Dauphine Street mansion, opening to the courtyard. There were far better rooms in the house. The distance to the bedrooms, kitchen, and parlor was the only thing that had saved him, thus far, from discovery.

He pulled his black jeans out from under the coffee table, snatched his T-shirt off the top of a bookcase, and dressed, staring at the woman on the couch.

How the hell do I get her out of here?

"Need some help?"

Khaos jumped at the sound of his aunt Desiree's voice. In his haste to escape his misadventure, he'd completely missed that the interior door leading to a long, dark hallway was wide open.

Desiree stood in the shadows, tucked away from the rays of the sun, an amused grin spread from ear to ear.

He ignored her, grabbing a throw blanket and tossing it over the still-sleeping woman. "No. I've got this," he said as he cast about for the woman's clothes.

"Over there." Desiree pointed to the far side of the room. "Doesn't look like she was wearing much."

Khaos wasn't in the mood for Desiree's cheek. Normally, he loved bantering with his aunt, but this wasn't the moment.

She giggled behind him as he grabbed the microscopic

dress and bright green thong underwear. "I could kill her for you. That would solve two problems: I'm hungry and Greer is bustling over our heads as we speak."

Khaos shot her a surprised look. "She's awake at this hour?"

"You know very well that she and Theron stay up all night when she returns."

"I don't need to know about my parents' extracurriculars." He shook his head, while Desiree laughed again. "Besides, shouldn't you be asleep yourself?"

She shrugged a freckled shoulder. "Apparently, vampire insomnia is a real thing. If you close the windows, I can help you dress her. Then you can whisk her out through the courtyard. Do you even know this one's name?"

Khaos shut his eyes, rubbing them with a knuckle in exasperation. "No, Auntie Des, I do not."

"Close the window and let me help."

Khaos didn't even look at her. He went to the window, shutting the curtains, knowing full well if there was anyone in the house who was always on his side, it was Auntie Des.

Desiree was one of his mother's closest friends, a foursome of women known as The Casket Girls. She'd been a vampire for three hundred years, living in the mansion with her vampire love, Jaxon. Desiree was a formidable woman, a survivor who'd led a horrific life back in France, but who became a fighter. She was the toughest woman he knew, besides his mom, and not because she was a vampire, but because she had the spirit of an army battalion.

Before he could turn around, Desiree was seated alongside the woman, brushing her hair from her face and cooing soft words. "Time to rise, my dear," she said as the woman stirred.

Khaos knew her compassion came from a hard life, the life she'd lived in Paris as a mortal. Desiree didn't begrudge him his many lovers, she only asked him one thing: make sure the women he bedded knew upfront there were no strings attached. She'd warned if he didn't do this one thing for her, she'd rip out his throat.

Despite his hedonistic ways, he'd always done as Desiree asked.

Desiree had the woman up, sitting on the edge of the couch, the blanket wrapped around her before Khaos could hand her the clothes.

Desiree took the wadded-up dress, smiling up at him. "Run to the kitchen. Get a glass of water and a pastry for Marisol, then hurry back."

Marisol. The name didn't ring a bell, but Khaos did as Desiree said, sprinting down the hallway to gather the items, then sprinting back again, all in the span of three minutes.

During that time, Desiree had helped Marisol into her dress. The two women were laughing and chatting like old friends when Khaos jogged back into the room, a glass of water in one hand, a cheese Danish in the other. The household entertained human friends and friends who were not quite human but who needed nourishment, so the kitchen was always stocked with fresh food.

Marisol took the water but waved off the Danish. "I'm good, thanks," she said between sips. "My car will be here in five minutes." She gulped down the rest of the water, handing the glass back to Khaos, who stood like a statue, never knowing how to act in these situations, although he'd been in this exact situation a thousand times.

"Thanks, Desiree." Marisol leaned over, kissing Des on the cheek before she turned her attention back to Khaos. "And thank you for a super fun night." She stretched on tiptoes, planting a quick kiss on Khaos's mouth. Before he could respond, she was gone, out the doors to the courtyard, never to be seen by him again.

The relief he felt was nearly palpable. He glanced at Des, who stood with her arms folded and that same sly grin spread across her face. "Maybe I'll tell Greer after all. I am her best friend, and keeping secrets is not something we do."

Khaos knew she was messing with him. He cocked his

head to the side, narrowing his eyes as he set down the empty glass and uneaten pastry. "I suppose you could. If you can reach Mom before I reach you."

Desiree squealed as she took off out the door and down the long hall. Khaos sprinted after her, laughing as he ran. The worry of the morning was gone now, and he was back to being his lackadaisical self. Something he excelled at. Nothing ever bothered him for long. Once a crisis had been averted, the memory of it left him completely, a reason why he rarely ever learned a lesson. What did anything matter to him? As the adopted son of the demon prince, Theron, and a demigoddess, nothing could touch him. Hell, his grandmother was Persephone. Khaos could get away with murder if he wanted.

AD BRAZEAU

CHAPTER TWO

Desiree beat him to the parlor, but only because he let her. She was heading toward Greer, who could almost always be found in the parlor, her favorite room in the house.

Khaos hadn't seen his mom in three months.

Long before his time, Greer had made a deal with Hades, her stepfather, to save Theron from certain death. Hades demanded that Greer spend three months of every year in the Underworld with her mother Persephone. Greer had adhered to this ever since.

The train of Desiree's blood-red gown swished around the edge of the doorframe as she fled through the door, disappearing inside.

Khaos entered right on her heels, but his forward momentum halted the second he slammed into the back of his father, Theron.

Theron was not a small man. Six foot five with a body as solid as an ancient redwood, he wasn't easy to overtake. When Khaos, nearly the same height as his father with similar muscle mass, slammed into him, Theron didn't budge an inch. He simply reached behind him to edge

Khaos away like he was nothing more than a child.

"Sorry, Father," Khaos said as he moved to the side.

Desiree had taken a seat on the sofa, which had been reupholstered in yellow silk. The room was darkened for her, the curtains to the verandah drawn, so she could sit and visit safely. Rather than turn on the overhead chandelier, the room was aglow in candlelight, the four sconces on the wall lit along with a cluster of tapers in the middle of the coffee table.

Greer rose from her seat in the matching yellow silk chair, her arms outstretched, her beautiful face illuminated by the flickering light. She wore a more modern style than Desiree, who preferred to dress in the 1700s style that was fashionable when she was human. At least she did when at home. This morning, Greer wore a cotton sundress in her favorite color, green. Her arms were bare with thin, layered bracelets as her only jewelry. She was barefoot, not unusual for her, and she looked no older than a child, which Khaos supposed she technically still was, having been made immortal by Persephone when she was only twenty-four. Greer wasn't afflicted with vampirism as were Desiree and Jaxon, she was made immortal by a goddess, given an elixir of eternal life so Persephone would never have to be without her.

Khaos, as well, would forever remain a young man. As a demon, his body froze in time once he reached full maturity, which for a human was somewhere around twenty-five. The same as his father, Theron.

Although once a demon prince, Theron had been cursed by Hades after getting caught with his tongue down Persephone's throat. He'd been cursed to live a sort of half-life as a demon-vampire hybrid. Still a demon, from then on, he would crave blood and burn in the sun. The fateful tryst with Persephone occurred long before Theron met Greer.

Greer jumped into her son's arms, and he held her tight around the waist while she squeezed him about the neck. "I missed you so much," she said, holding on for a minute, then released him to step away. There was a familiar look in her eye as she appraised him.

"What is it?" Khaos asked.

Greer glanced in Theron's direction. Theron cleared his throat as he moved alongside Greer, his massive hand enveloping her tiny one. Greer placed her free hand on his arm. "Let me handle this."

Khaos slid a glance toward Desiree, who sat as still as stone, a bemused smile spread across her face. She knew this was going to happen, that's why she hadn't gone to bed. Khaos was about to receive a dressing down from his parents, and Desiree just couldn't help but observe. Khaos stuck his tongue out at her, her smile widening.

"Khaos, we've turned a blind eye to your"—Greer paused—"your escapades. But, truly, your womanizing, drinking, and general debauchery have gone on long enough. You're a grown man."

"Demon, actually," Desiree interrupted.

Theron pursed his lips, shooting her a glance over his shoulder. "Be helpful or leave."

Desiree snickered behind her hand.

Khaos turned his full attention to his parents. There was only one way to get out of this, and that was to fake contrition as he'd done a hundred times in the past several years. He clasped his hands in front of him, lowering his head by a degree. "What do you want me to do, Mother?"

Greer smiled up at Theron, who merely stared at Khaos with a wry look. "See, he can be reasonable." Looking back at her son, she said, "It's time for you to become a more responsible man. It's time, my son, that you become a productive member of society."

Khaos wanted to laugh. He had to muster every last ounce of his willpower not to snort in delight. A productive member of society? This was a major familial sticking point. While the rest of them all provided some sort of service, Khaos never saw the point. They were supernatural beings, every one of them. They didn't have to lift a finger to run their bath water. Why did they all feel it necessary to *help* mortals?

Desiree, Jaxon, and Theron were all vigilantes of sorts. Stalking the streets of New Orleans and the surrounding environs ridding the city of evil-doers, human and otherwise. Greer did charity work at the local hospital, as she was the only one of the four who could be outdoors during daylight hours. Even Fosette and Lucian, members of their extended family, and a pair of formidable witches, did good by providing healing to people who asked for it.

"Khaos does his part," Desiree interrupted, again. "He's given many a woman a night she'll never forget."

Theron closed his eyes. "Desiree, don't you have anything better to do?"

"Not really," was her sassy retort.

"Des, dear"—Greer turned to her friend—"please give us a few moments alone."

Desiree crossed her arms across her chest. "Fine. I need to get some sleep anyway." She rose from the sofa, her arms still folded tight, winked a wicked green eye at Khaos, and swept from the room.

Greer turned back to Khaos and smiled. "I want you to come to the hospital with me. And I want you to meet someone."

"Mom, no." Khaos shook his head. "I can't be around sick people. It gives me the creeps, and I don't have any interest in meeting a woman you've picked out for me."

"She isn't a mortal woman, Khaos. Do you think I'd pick a mortal for you? I doubt there's a human alive who could deal with you for long. No." Greer shook her head, a soft smile on her lips. "The lady I have in mind is truly remarkable."

Khaos looked at her like she was crazy. "So, this is an arranged marriage sort of thing? Are you out of your mind? Absolutely not."

A low, menacing growl emanated from somewhere deep

within Theron. His eyes glowed as he stared bullets at his son. "Don't speak to your mother that way. This isn't up for debate. You'll do as we ask, or you'll find somewhere else to sow your oats."

Khaos's mouth dropped open. His parents had been unhappy with his behavior for some time, but they had never towed such a hard line with him before. He was practically speechless.

After a couple of seconds, he sighed like a spoiled child. "Are you serious? If I don't go to the hospital with Mom, and if I don't meet the woman you've picked out for me, you'll kick me out? This isn't the middle ages, you can't just tell me who I'm going to have a relationship with."

"Stop being so dramatic." Theron's voice thundered through the room. "You're not a child any longer, Khaos. Stop acting like one."

"Fine. I won't give you the satisfaction of kicking me out. I'm kicking myself out." Khaos stomped on the floor. "That's not what I meant. I meant that I'm leaving."

He turned on his heel and lumbered out the door. Greer called out to him, but his mind was made up. If they no longer wanted him as he was, then he'd leave. The last thing Khaos would do was change for anyone.

His room was one of the larger in the mansion. The bed, a California king, sat in front of one long wall, the black duvet rumpled near the foot. He hadn't slept in his bed in several days. He wanted to sleep then, was so tired he very nearly laid down, but he wouldn't give in to the desire for comfort. Not yet. He meant what he'd said to his parents, he would leave. Or at least go through the motions of packing his things, giving them plenty of time to come to their senses and apologize.

So, he did just that. He pulled out a canvas duffel, then began riffling through drawers, yanking out underwear and socks. He threw open his closet doors, grabbing a few pairs of his favorite designer denim along with several T-shirts, button-downs, and whatever would fit in the bag. He put on fresh clothes— a crisp pair of black pants and a thin gray sweater—then slipped his feet into brand-new Ferragamo loafers.

By the time he was finished, several minutes had gone by without anyone appearing at the wide-open bedroom door.

Khaos stepped into the hall, but no one was about. He didn't even hear voices.

Whatever.

He decided to give it a little more time for his parents to come to their senses and went into his bathroom for his toiletries. Once everything was zipped into the duffel, he threw on a leather jacket, glancing at his Cartier watch. Ten minutes had passed. No one was coming.

Fine. I don't need them or this place.

For effect, he pulled the duvet off the bed and threw it on the ground, then stomped out of the room.

It was true that he didn't need his parents. He was a capable being with his own bank account and his bank cards safely inside his wallet. There was plenty of money to get an apartment, furniture, and everything he needed. Maybe this would even be better. There would be no more sneaking around and no more sneaking women out of the mansion.

The halls were silent as Khaos made his way through the creamy stone passageways and out to the wrought iron stairway.

By the time he was outside the courtyard gates, sitting inside his Verde Lamborghini Aventador SVJ, his spirits were considerably higher. Freedom was what he'd craved all along.

Next stop—the bank.

CHAPTER THREE

Jeanne Antoinette Poisson liked to keep to the shadows. The shadows were the perfect place to watch and not be seen. She didn't need to be seen, didn't want to be seen. The fewer people who knew she existed, the better.

Love and friendship were not words in her vocabulary. Best to live like a nun.

Music thumped from the front of the house, a dull rumble by the time it reached her, ensconced in the expansive back office where she hibernated during the daylight hours. The room had no windows. Neither did the hallway that led to her upstairs apartment. This made walking from her home to her job without burning to a crisp, a breeze.

She purchased this building forty years ago when real estate in the Quarter could be had for a song. A song was about all she'd had at the time after losing her cache of jewels to the Comte St. Germain years ago. Escaping the Comte and his nightmare way of life was all she'd cared about then. She'd fled New Orleans back to Europe, where she'd found shelter with a strange group of vampires who lived in the Catacombs underneath Paris. It was a filthy life, the smell of dirt a constant, the sound of skittering rats her only music. But she'd felt safe down there under the earth, hidden away from the eyes of men. Men had only led her astray. After the Comte and what he'd done to her, all she wanted was peace.

After eighty years, she felt secure enough to leave her underground haven. Word had reached her that the Comte was dead, his ashes scattered to the four winds. Before she knew what she was doing, she was traveling back across the expanse, back to New Orleans, the site of her turmoil. She told herself there was something about New Orleans she'd always loved, but the reality was, she wanted to make sure the Comte was gone, and it appeared he was. What's more, she wanted to find her jewels. They'd never hit either the auction circuit or the black market, which meant he'd likely squirreled them away. She hadn't found them yet, but she also wasn't going to give up.

The bar she'd opened on the bottom floor of the building she'd purchased wasn't much, but in the Quarter, it didn't have to be. The crappiness was part of the charm. She named the place Noir, painted the interior black, added blood-red cloths over the tables, found some antique, barely functioning chandeliers at a yard sale, and threw some goth favorites inside the jukebox. Within days of opening, Noir had become a hotspot with the local goth crowd, and now, forty years later, Noir was a tourist destination. The bar was packed every night of the week from early evening to close. Antoinette was a woman in a comfortable position. Still, she wanted those jewels.

"Antoinette." Deena, the manager of Noir, knocked on the office door.

"Come," Antoinette called.

Deena, her six-foot frame ducking to clear the two-hundred-year-old door jamb, entered the room. Deena was a godsend. It was because of her the bar ran like a well-oiled machine. Antoinette didn't know what she'd do if she ever left, which was why she paid her well above the going rate.

"There's some guy causing problems out front." She meant inside the bar. "Mark doesn't get here until six. He's having issues with his sitter again."

Antoinette groaned. Mark was the bouncer, another great find. He was a single dad who could never seem to find the right babysitter. Antoinette had tried to help him find someone suitable on numerous occasions to no avail. It wasn't Deena's job to handle rough guests, and it certainly wasn't the job of the two female bartenders, both in their early twenties. Antoinette could have thrown the guy out with her pinky finger, but there were two problems: one was that no one who worked for her knew her secret, and the other was that the sun hadn't yet set. The whole front of the bar was glass with floor-to-ceiling windows that were uncovered when the place was open.

"I'll call the police." Antoinette picked up the phone.

"Just a reminder that the last time we did that, the police didn't get here for almost an hour."

"Shit." Antoinette put the phone down.

"Yep." Deena placed her hands on her hips. "The guy is pretty massive, like in a muscular way. I'm not sure the four of us together could even get him out."

"What's he doing?"

"Drinking like it's his job and hitting on everything with tits that walks by. Not in the normal 'drunk guy in a bar' kind of way, but in the 'super creepy, gross' kind of way."

"Is there a difference?"

"Big difference. If you know, you know."

Antoinette had to laugh. "I guess I don't know."

"If you left the office once in a while you might gain some important drunk-guy intelligence."

"I think that's intelligence I can live without." Antoinette placed her hands on the desk. "Okay, I guess I have no choice but to intervene."

This had to be strategic. If Antoinette could stay in the shadows near the back of the bar, she may be able to get away with this. It wasn't like direct sunlight would cause her to burst into flames or anything, but she would burn. She might even smoke a little, but she wasn't entirely sure. She hadn't experimented with sunlight in a very long time. But explaining why her skin was smoking to her employees and the patrons of the bar was not something she wanted to do. No one knew what she was, and that was how she liked it.

Antoinette rose from her chair. "After you." She motioned for Deena to lead the way.

"What's the play here?" Deena asked over her shoulder as she stepped out the door and into the dark hallway.

"The play is just to get this guy out of here. How many people are out front?"

"It's early, so not many. Maybe half the tables are taken, and most of the seats at the bar."

That wasn't many for Noir. Antoinette was at least grateful for that. The fewer people to witness a scene that would undoubtedly get ugly, the better.

"I'm going to wing it." Antoinette may not have experience with drunk guys, but she did have experience with scary men, men who were powerful in one way or another. It may have been a long time since she'd been in an unfortunate position, but something told her the instincts would return. Sort of like riding a bike, as humans say.

Deena strode to the end of the hall, turning the knob to the door marked *Employees Only*, and walked through to the sunlit bar.

Antoinette took a deep breath, following her through. Before she'd even closed the door behind her, she heard the man in question. He was yelling his phone number at someone. Probably someone who wasn't giving him the time of day by the tone of his voice. She almost felt sorry for the guy. He clearly wasn't having a good day.

She decided to leave the employee door open in case she needed to beat a quick retreat. The man wasn't difficult to spot. In one hand he held on to an empty whisky glass with a tight grip. Antoinette was sure it would shatter any minute.

The other hand waved around as he stumbled, seemingly talking to no one. The early-day patrons in their sneakers and Tommy Bahama shirts were giving him a wide berth. If she didn't get this guy on his way, he'd scare off the tourists.

Luckily, he was ambling toward the back of the bar, right toward her. Deena took up a position next to Antoinette, her tall, athletic body a good deterrent to violence, or so Antoinette hoped.

The man stumbled forward, and Antoinette put up her hand. He came to a stop right in front of her, swaying as he tried to stay on his feet.

"Sir." Antoinette tried to puff herself up, but she could only make herself appear so big. Unlike Deena, she was only around five foot two and so slight that the man in front of her could have thrown her over his shoulder in a heartbeat. Her true power was preternatural, but again, she couldn't let anyone see that side of her.

"Sir, please." Antoinette looked the man over. Deena wasn't wrong, he was massive. Much taller than Deena and about as wide as two normal men. This guy was a wall of solid muscle. His hair was jet black, his eyes an arresting hazel green. She'd expect a man this size to be angular and lean, but his bone structure was unusual, almost feminine, beautiful really. Otherworldly.

That's when she knew. Drunk guy wasn't human.

"I know you." The man narrowed his eyes as he tried to focus.

Deena snickered next to her.

"I doubt that very much."

"No, I've seen you before. In a portrait."

Antoinette's stomach clenched.

Shit.

In the early days, Antoinette had been recognized often. How could she not be? Nearly as famous as Marie Antoinette, her face, immortalized in oils, had been seen the world over, and her exploits spoken about on nearly every continent. As the years had slipped away and she'd gotten farther away from the decadent woman she'd once been, she'd stopped being recognized. Adopting modern hairstyles and clothing choices had helped disguise her. But if this man wasn't human, as Antoinette suspected, he might have been alive when she was mortal. He could also just be a history buff. The only way to find out was to get to him alone. Of course, the other alternative, the smart one, was to make this guy think she was no one and get him the hell out of her bar.

She laughed, shaking her head as she did so. "Boy, you are drunk."

Deena's snicker turned into a full-blown laugh.

The man fixed her in a stare that made her squirm. Why did he make her squirm?

"I never stay drunk for long. It's been a shitty day."

She softened her stance, her neck craning to look him in the eye. "Look, we all have bad days, but I can't have you in here harassing my female staff and customers. No matter what's going on with you, that isn't cool."

He opened his mouth to say something, then closed it again. Antoinette could tell from his steadier stance that he was sobering up.

Definitely not human.

"I can see I made a mistake. My apologies." He held out the whisky glass, and Deena took it from him. "I'll leave you."

Something about the way he said *I'll leave you* sounded so pathetic that Antoinette nearly asked him to stay. But she couldn't do that. Not without a bouncer to help should this guy start slamming drinks again.

She nodded.

He kept eye contact for one more second, then turned, much steadier on his feet now, and walked out the bar's front door, into the sunlit day.

Not a vampire, then.

"Okay, that was super weird," Deena said.

"Super weird," Antoinette agreed. Part of putting on an

act that she was a regular woman was using the current vernacular, hate it though she did. She glanced at Deena. "I'm heading back to the invoices. Let me know if he comes back."

"You got it, boss."

Antoinette retreated to the safety zone of her dimly lit office. She tried to get back to the books, but all she could think about was the man who'd stumbled around her bar.

What was he?

She felt unnerved. In the forty years she'd been back, she'd seen a few other creatures like herself, but they'd kept to themselves, as had she. This man was unlike anything she'd encountered, and that could be quite bad.

AD BRAZEAU

CHAPTER FOUR

By the time Khaos made his way back to his car, he was completely sober. This was one of the downsides to being a demon, his body metabolized any alcohol he drank within a couple of hours, sometimes less.

He sat in the driver's seat, the black leather enveloping him like a soft hug. He nestled farther in, resting his head against the headrest, looking out on what was about to become nighttime in the Quarter. People were already stumbling from one sidewalk to another, women in short skirts and dresses, beads hanging around their necks, plastic cups gripped in manicured hands, giggling and talking in high-pitched voices while men in groups of three and four whooped and hollered in much the same inebriated state. A good time would be had by all in the Quarter tonight.

He cracked the window, zydeco music from a nearby club pouring onto the streets. Khaos admired the architecture, ignoring the bleached blonde precariously balanced on her platform shoes as she kept trying to dip down to catch his eye. She stood on the corner with her friends, two of them arguing, one of them barely on her feet, and so early in the evening. Khaos wasn't in the mood tonight. Instead, he glanced up, taking in the wrought iron balconies above him, some with little patio sets, some teeming with plants, wondering what the lives of the people who lived within were like. This was something he did often when he started feeling blue. He would walk or drive through the Quarter or the Garden District, staring at the beautiful homes and imagining the wonderful lives of the locals.

He'd originally been content to leave the home of his parents, happy to finally strike out on his own. It wasn't until he got to the bank that he discovered his account, his father's account, really, had been closed. Khaos had nothing more than the clothes he'd packed, his watch, his car, the title of which was in his name only, and about four hundred dollars in cash. The logical thing would have been to return home. With an apology and a promise to behave better, his mother would always welcome him home with open arms. But he didn't want to go home. He wanted to prove to them that he didn't need them, and he didn't feel as if he needed to change his ways. He was young after all. His parents should expect a little wildness, a little sowing of oats, and all that.

No, Khaos didn't feel bad for his past behavior. He didn't live in a household of saints, except for his mother, so why should they all expect him to be such an angel? There was only one thing he felt bad for at the moment, and that was acting like such an ass at Noir.

Even in his most drunken state, he'd never leered at women like some disgusting lecher. He didn't have to. Women came to him. Much like the blonde still staring at him from the street corner, all he had to do was lie in wait. He was a bit disgusted with himself. After having found that he was essentially homeless, he'd gone a bit overboard. And then there was that woman.

She was familiar to him almost instantly. The plump cheeks, the full cupid's bow mouth, the straight nose, and the delicate widow's peak. Her posture was regal, formal.

She'd tried to slouch a little, to drop her shoulders in a modern way, but even in her jeans, she failed to look modern. And Khaos knew a vampire when he saw one. He lived with vampires and was raised by them. There was Desiree and Jaxon and his father, a demon-vampire hybrid.

That was why Khaos had moved to the back of the bar as soon as he saw her. He didn't want to put her in direct sunlight.

Khaos shook his head. He had other concerns at the moment, such as the intoxicated girl gang staring him down.

The brazen blonde had had enough of being ignored. Bold in her drunkenness, she'd pounded over to the side of his car, slamming her rather large hands near the edge of the rolled-up window. "Hey, you!" she practically screamed through the glass. She giggled, then hiccupped, covering her mouth with her hand. "Oops, that was loud." She tried to smile in an alluring way, dropping her shoulder so the strap of her tank top would slip down, exposing the tops of her pushed-up bosom.

Khaos closed his eyes. He didn't want to deal with this. Not now. He cracked the window, revving the engine. "Step back before you get hurt."

Her mouth dropped open. The fact that she was being rejected had dawned on her and she didn't like it one bit. "Don't you think you're hot shit?" She kicked the side of his car with her plastic shoe, probably scraping a bit of paint.

Khaos kept his cool. He wasn't going to lose it with a woman, and certainly not with a woman under as little control as this one.

He fixed her in his most vicious stare. "Move away from my vehicle."

That did it. She moved, stepping back onto the sidewalk, out of harm's way. She thrust her strap back onto her shoulder as her friends clustered around her, throwing him death stares as if he were the asshole in the situation.

There was only one situation in which he'd recently been the asshole, and he intended on offering a sincere apology.

After moving his Lambo over a couple of blocks, he didn't trust the drunk girl gang not to key his car, he made his way back through the narrow streets of the Quarter toward Noir. He realized he may not even be granted admittance, but he had to try. Not only did he want to apologize to the staff, but he had to talk to the proprietress once again.

He had two working theories on who she might be, and there was only one way to find out.

With the sun almost fully set, tourists were out in the Quarter in full force, drinking, carousing, laughing, and tripping over uneven pavement. Music and A/C poured out of bars and clubs. This close to Bourbon Street, there was that ever-present unpleasant aroma, a mixture of sour alcohol and sour vomit. On a Saturday night, the smell was nearly unbearable.

Thank the gods, he was going in the opposite direction. On Chartres, he ducked into Noir. The place was packed with people. In the twenty minutes he'd been gone, the tourist crowd had evaporated in favor of the goths. Every chair at every table was full, as was every seat at the bar. The dance floor was crowded with dancers swaying to Siouxsie and the Banshees. Nearly every patron wore black, some of the outfits more elaborate than others. Most of the women wore black dresses with black combat boots, thick black eyeliner, and dyed black hair, while most of the men wore black pants and shirts, also with the requisite combat boots and eyeliner. A few took the goth look a bit more seriously. One lady, probably in her mid-thirties, wore an exquisite black lace dress, a satin corset cinched tightly around her waist. Above her head, she carried an open, purple lace parasol, and instead of the combat boots, she wore purple Victorian-style buckle shoes. This lady didn't come to play.

A young woman grazed Khaos's elbow. He turned to find a baby bat, probably barely out of high school, gazing up at him, her big blue eyes lined in thick black kohl. "Excuse me." She batted long, fake eyelashes as her blood-red lips split into a wide grin.

Khaos was too smart to take the bait. He was pretty sure that was exactly what this girl was. "You should be home studying for your math final," he yelled over the music.

She rolled her eyes and moved on.

"Oh, hell no." He heard the woman whom he'd encountered earlier before he saw her.

She must have been the manager, as she seemed to bustle around doing a little of everything. Her height was impressive, at least six feet by Khaos's estimation. Her hair was cut short, close to her head, and her brown skin was flawless without a stitch of makeup on.

Khaos put up his hands. "I have come in peace. I've sobered up and I just wanted to apologize." Apologizing was not something he did often. Why he felt so compelled to do it now had everything to do with the petite woman he'd once seen hanging somewhere in a museum.

The tall woman folded her arms across her chest. "Bullshit. No one sobers up that fast. You drank half a bottle of whiskey. You should be puking in a gutter right now."

Khaos straightened his shoulders. "Clearly, I'm not. You have experience with drunks—do I seem drunk now?" He looked her right in the eye.

She narrowed hers. "I suppose not. That doesn't change the fact that you behaved like a stupid fuck, and we don't want you here."

He nodded. "I get it. I do. I'll finish my apology tour and leave." He glanced over his shoulder. "Don't you usually have a bouncer at the door?" Khaos had been to Noir on a few other occasions, and there was usually a beefy guy sitting on a stool checking IDs.

"Not tonight. He had a situation."

Khaos looked back at her. He didn't usually do things for other people, but a thought occurred to him. If he was going to try his hand at this independent life thing, he was going to need a job. A job at Noir would get him closer to the petite brunette.

"Let me do it," he said.

"What?" The woman threw a towel over her shoulder, laughing as she did so.

"Let me work the door. I doubt it's rocket science, and you need someone to keep an eye on things. By my count, four women work here, and not a single man. Now, I'm not discounting how strong any of you might be, but you and I both know the bar will be safer with a big dude at the door."

She glanced over at the bar where one of the bartenders was asking if she needed help. She held up her hand. "I'm not sure you're the big dude for the job."

"Do you have anyone else coming in?"

"No."

"Then it won't hurt to stick me out there. If it goes well, and you need help again in the future, you can give me a call. No harm, no foul."

She sucked her lip into her mouth as she worked the idea in her mind. Khaos could tell when someone was mulling.

"Fine," she said. "Just for tonight. I can give you a percentage of the tips, plus a percentage of the night's take. If you fuck around once, you're out. I'll call the cops. Deal?"

Khaos raised his eyebrows and smiled. "Deal."

"Deena."

"Khaos. With a K."

"Of course, you are."

Khaos laughed, bowing his head and retreating to the stool at the door. For the next several hours he'd keep Noir safe and make a little money. Hopefully, he'd also get another chance to talk to the woman he knew was somewhere in the building.

CHAPTER FIVE

"Hey, boss." Deena knocked on the open door.

"Hey, come in." Antoinette was standing at the cabinet, filing receipts.

"That guy from earlier is back."

"No." Antoinette reached for the phone on her desk. "Time to call the police."

"Wait. He came back totally sober, wanting to apologize."

"What?" Antoinette, her hand resting on the edge of her desk, looked at Deena. "He apologized?"

"Yeah, and he's working the door."

"Excuse me?" Now Antoinette looked at Deena like she was crazy. It was strange enough that the out-of-control drunk had returned to apologize, but then Deena had put him on the door?

Deena cracked a rare smile, putting up a hand. "I know. I know you're going to say I must be insane, but, seriously, Antoinette, it's the weirdest thing. He's dead sober. In the thirty-three years I've been on this earth, I've seen a lot of drunk people, and I've never, not once, seen someone go from raging alchy to stone-cold sober so quickly. But I'll be damned if it didn't happen. And the fact of the matter is, Mark isn't here, the house is packed, and we need a muscle man running interference."

Antoinette leaned against the desk. Deena didn't know what she did. The previously drunk man wasn't a man, but Antionette had to feign shock at the fact that he'd sobered up so quickly. "Wow, I've never heard of such a thing. But I trust your judgment. I'll step out in a few to take my measure of him."

"Sounds like a plan, boss." Deena half-saluted on her way back out the door.

"Wait, what's his name?"

Deena tossed a look over her shoulder. "Khaos, with a K."

Khaos sounded like a demon name. Antoinette groaned. She didn't know much about demons, but what she did know wasn't positive. Khaos may very well bring the roof down with his mayhem. So, Antoinette prepared to go out onto the floor for the second time in thirty minutes. Before that day, the last time she'd been in the front of the house was over two months ago, and that was only to sign for a delivery that had come to the front door instead of the back.

Antionette walked to the mirror hanging over the fireplace mantle. The mirror was French, nearly as old as she was, with gilt edging and beveled glass. She wasn't sure why it mattered to her, but she took stock of her appearance for the first time in a century. Her hair, a soft brown color she always considered mousy, needed brushing. Instead of doing that, she wound it between her fingers and twirled it into a low bun. She pinned it in place at the nape of her neck, pulling out some face-framing tendrils. She pinched her pale cheeks, bringing up some much-needed color. There wasn't much else to be done, as she didn't have a bag of cosmetics at her disposal. Makeup always seemed like more of a bother than it was worth, but now she longed for some mascara, and maybe even a lip gloss.

She shook her head, laughing at herself as she stepped

away from the looking glass. Who cared what she looked like? A demon named Khaos was the last creature she wanted to attract.

Antoinette stepped from her safe hidey-hole into the soft light of Noir. The house was packed with gothically-clad bodies, many of them swaying to *Book of Love* issuing from the jukebox. She stayed near the office door, stretching on her tiptoes to see over the dancers between her and the front entrance. Sure enough, there was the demon, sitting on the bouncer's stool, checking IDs as more people streamed inside.

Antoinette edged around the room, placing a hand on the dark mahogany bar as she watched.

"Hey, girl, you want a drink?" Carrie, one of her bartenders, the one with the full-sleeve tattoos, asked over Antoinette's shoulder.

"No, thanks," Antoinette said. "I'm just checking on our new friend."

"He seems cool now, like it never happened. He apologized and everything."

"Yeah, that's what Deena said." Antoinette hated using words like *yeah*. She tried not to cringe.

Carrie went back to serving drinks alongside her counterpart, Nicole. The ladies would be slammed until closing. They would also be rewarded handsomely. Not only were their nightly tips insane, but Antoinette made sure to make the deal even sweeter to retain good employees. Mark was the only employee she'd had trouble with in years, and the trouble wasn't his fault. If he left her, Antoinette would make sure he had a good severance and an even better recommendation.

She trailed her hand along the waxy bar for as long as she could, as bodies were cramming the front of it, and walked over to the entrance. She stood behind the massive back of the demon who called himself Khaos. His head was bent over IDs, seeming to take real stock of birth years before waving people in. Many women, at least three of them drop-dead gorgeous, tried to get his attention by leaning bosoms into his view, laughing loudly, which was very un-goth-like, or by simply clearing their throats, but he never looked at one longer than it took to ascertain if the photos and the faces matched.

Deena came up behind her fast, her bar towel, as always, thrown over a shoulder. She glanced at Antoinette, then held up a hand. "We're at capacity. Any more and the fire marshal will be all over my ass." She said this to Khaos, who immediately held out an arm the size of a tree trunk to stop the flow of patrons. Deena continued, "If they want to wait, they line up against the side of the building and you can bring people in as others leave. One for one."

Khaos stood, nodding. "Got it." He turned to block the doorway. "At capacity. Line up," he barked in a commanding voice.

The crowd immediately fell back. They didn't have to be told twice by him. Some of them dispersed, not willing to wait when there were other places to drink. Others did as they were told, lining up to wait their turn.

Khaos resumed his seat, arms crossed across his chest, his back still to Antoinette. When Deena walked off, Antoinette moved into the doorway he'd previously occupied, feeling like an ant next to an elephant. She didn't fill the space as he had.

His head turned toward her, jet-black hair falling over his brow. He pushed it back, piercing her with those hazel eyes. "Hey," he said.

"Hello," she said, a little too formally, then covered with an added, "Hey."

He laughed a low, deep rumble. "You can cut the act with me. I know you're not of this time. Anyway, I was going to apologize to you on my tour, but Deena needed somebody at the door ASAP. I'm truly sorry for my earlier behavior. Like I said, it's been a crap day, but that's no excuse."

She ignored his comment about putting on an act. "Thank you for the apology. And thanks for helping us with the door. We have someone, and I'm sure he'll be back tomorrow night, but the gesture is appreciated."

He nodded. "So, are you going to confirm what I already know, or are we going to keep pretending?"

Antoinette jerked around, ignoring Khaos's question. Her preternatural ears picked up someone in the back rooms, but all the employees were within her view and there was no way Deena would let someone go through the door to Antoinette's office. "What the hell?"

"What is it?" Khaos half stood, half leaned against the stool.

"Someone's in my office," she said as she strained her ears to listen.

Khaos leaped forward. "Someone who shouldn't be." It wasn't a question but a statement.

Antoinette grabbed his shirt sleeve. "I can handle this."

"Fine." Khaos backed down but didn't resume his seat.

Antionette took off through the bodies, careful not to walk too fast. She needed to appear casual, like she was just walking back to her office, nothing amiss. She plastered a fake smile on her face as she nodded at patrons and Deena, who was looking at her quizzically.

Right before Antoinette wrenched open the door marked *Employees Only,* she heard a crash so loud it startled everyone in the club. She opened the door and ran down the hall, footsteps behind her. Khaos overtook her, flying past her and into her office.

Antoinette was right behind him. When she rounded the corner and crossed the threshold, she had to take another step back as a woman she'd never seen before nearly mowed her over. The woman, her long white hair flowing behind her, held out a hand and shot Antoinette square in the chest with a blast of blue light.

Antoinette doubled over, gasping for breath as strong

hands gripped her around the waist.

"Breathe," Khaos said over her. "That witchy bitch blasted me, too. She was feistier than she looked, but she's gone now."

"A witch?" Antoinette took two painful breaths, then straightened up, stepping out of Khaos's grasp.

"Yeah. I was raised around witches, so I'm familiar. You okay?"

Antoinette barely registered what he said as she took in her office. The drawers of her Louis XIV desk were open, the contents strewn across the floor. The drawers of her filing cabinet were in the same state. Her antique Turkish rug was thrown to the side of the room, and most heartbreaking of all, her cherished French mirror, a true antique gifted to her by her lover King Louis XV, was in pieces, shattered across the wood floor.

"No," she muttered, collapsing into the nearest chair.

Khaos stood in the doorway but was pushed inside by Deena. "Antoinette, what the hell happened?" She was framed by the light from the hall as she took in the destruction of the room.

Antoinette had to cover fast. Not only would her way of life be in danger if any mortals found out about her, but those mortals who had become her friends would also be in danger. "It was a junkie, by the looks of him. He broke in through the courtyard. Probably looking for cash." She gestured between herself and Khaos. "We scared him off."

"I'll call the police and file a report."

"No," Antoinette said, a little too loudly. "I'll do it. I need to see if anything is missing first. Please go back out and tell people the mirror fell off the wall. No need to alarm anyone else."

Deena looked down at her, a scowl marring her forehead. "Okay, but have Khaos check the courtyard gate. I want that secure before we leave you tonight."

"I'm on it," Khaos said.

"Okay, but I'll make sure to check your work." Deena

raised an eyebrow.

Khaos chuckled under his breath. "I wouldn't expect anything less."

Deena turned to leave but hesitated.

"It's okay, Deena. I've got it from here."

Deena nodded at Antoinette before slowly heading down the hallway.

Antoinette waited until she heard Deena shut the outer door, then cocked her head to the side. "Funny how a demon shows up in my bar the same night a witch destroys my office."

Khaos threw up his hands. "Hey, this had nothing to do with me. The witches I know are cool." He scowled. "So, you know I'm a demon. Are you going to finally admit what you are?"

"A vampire? I'm pretty sure you already knew that." She stood up to retrieve a broom from the closet.

"I clocked you the second I saw you," he said as she began to sweep up the glass from her irreplaceable mirror. "And I know you have to be one of two people. Deena called you Antoinette. I thought you might be Marie Antoinette, but your hair is too brown, so I'm going with the more logical answer. I told you I'd seen your portrait in a museum. You're Madame de Pompadour."

CHAPTER SIX

Antoinette stared at him, astonishment clear in her wide-open eyes and mouth. He knew he had her dead to rights.

"It's been over two hundred and fifty years since anyone called me that. I'm hoping you can keep my secret." Her eyes were big and brown, so soft and deep that Khaos almost felt something in his cold, dead heart.

"Of course I'll keep your secret. As long as you keep mine." Khaos meant what he said. He didn't often keep his promises, but he would keep this one.

"Sure, because telling people you're a demon would really make me look sane."

He laughed. "As sane as telling people you're the vampiric Madame de Pompadour."

Glass clinked as she continued to sweep up the broken pieces of mirror. "People around here would sooner believe in vampires than demons."

Khaos walked over to her, careful to not step on the larger pieces of glass, and took the broom to resume the sweeping while she moved to her desk.

"Why would a witch be searching your office? What could you have that she wants?" He watched her while he swept, studying her face for any tell. He may not have been good at most things, but he knew when someone was lying to him.

She pushed in the top drawer of her desk as her gaze seemed to catch on something. "Seriously?" Antoinette ignored his questions and instead crouched alongside the desk. "She pried up some of my floorboards."

Khaos leaned the broom against the fireplace mantle. "I ask again, what could the witch have been looking for? Surely, you have some idea." If someone had gone to the trouble of prying up thick, heavy floorboards, she must have something the witch wanted, and badly.

Antoinette's face was obscured as she pushed the boards back down with the palm of her hand. "I have no idea. I've lived here quietly for some time. I never go out. The only people I know are my employees."

"What do you mean you never go out? You have to feed, don't you?"

Antoinette stood up like a shot. "Thank you for your help, but you need to get back to working the entrance. I'm fine back here."

Khaos stepped back like she'd pushed him. "I'm sorry. My social skills aren't the best. My aunt says I don't know when to shut up. I guess she's right." He moved toward the door, then paused to take one last look at her. Her delicateness was heightened by the fragility of the antique desk she stood next to. There was something about this woman that made him want to sweep her into his arms. Not romantically, not in the way he was used to sweeping women off their feet, but protectively. As it was, there was nothing he could do. He couldn't very well force his protection on her. The only thing he could do was stand sentry at the door to her bar and keep an eye, and an ear, out for danger. "I'll be within earshot should you need anything."

Khaos went out back to do as Deena had asked. The courtyard gate was closed and all seemed quiet. He then made his way back to the front of the house, resuming his sentry at the door. The number of patrons inside Noir had not decreased by even one. He counted on his way through the crowd. The line out front, alongside the sidewalk on Chartres, hadn't changed either. People stood with arms folded across their chests, some leaning against the open black shutters, swaying to the music pouring outside.

The stool was hard, so Khaos didn't sit. Instead, he stood in much the same scowling position as the patrons out front: arms crossed, face sour, his mind working through what had happened inside Antoinette's office. He hadn't let on how impressed he'd been to be in her presence. Truth be told, he was a little starstruck. He'd never been starstruck before, not even when he'd bedded a world-famous movie star. Impressing a demon was hard, especially a demon whose mother had been one of the famous Casket Girls, the women who'd been brought to New Orleans in the early 1700s as brides for the locals. But to be in the presence of such an astounding historical figure, Khaos had been a little awed. Just a little. After all, his mother had lived in France, and the other Casket Girls were French.

He thought back many years to when he was a little demon. His parents had taken him to a portrait gallery filled with important French historical figures. Mother had lingered in front of Madame de Pompadour's painting. "She was really something," Greer had said as she gazed up at the lovely woman in the blush pink gown adorned with yards of ruffles. "She was politically savvy, smart, and a patron of the arts. She never lost her position, even after her sexual relationship with the king ended."

Khaos had been small then, barely up to his mother's hip bone, so this summation didn't mean much to him at the time, but as a fully grown man, he now understood why his mother had spoken with such favor.

Mother would fall over if I brought home the *Madame de Pompadour.*

Khaos chuckled at the thought. Of course, he wasn't on

speaking terms with his parents at the moment, so such a meeting would have to wait.

His thoughts turned to his aunt Fossette and uncle Lucian. Both were formidable witches who resided in the bayou. They had been alive as long as his mother, their lives extended by their powerful magic. Khaos spent a lot of time with them out in the bayou, so he knew a thing or two about witches. Witches didn't do things like breaking into the office of a vampire, at least not without a very good reason. Which is why he didn't buy Antoinette's cluelessness. She had to have some idea what the witch wanted with her, or from her.

Khaos couldn't blame Antoinette for being leery of him, especially after the spectacle he'd made of himself earlier in the day. She likely wanted to keep him as far away from her and her secrets as possible. And who could doubt that she was a mystery? Even mortals harbored confidences, and their lives were as dull as dishwater. He didn't doubt that the riddles locked in Madame's heart were both juicy and deadly.

And the thing about immortals? When you live forever, when there isn't much that can kill you, you tend to have patience on lock.

"How much longer?" The baby bat at the front of the line scowled at him, a crease marring her young forehead. A goth couple at the back of the line peeled off, heading toward the sights and smells of Bourbon Street.

"Could be minutes, could be tomorrow," Khaos said, the crowd inside Noir raucous behind him. He snarled, cocking an eyebrow as he gazed down Chartres. "Part of the fun is in the waiting. Makes the reward all the sweeter."

CHAPTER SEVEN

Antoinette stared down at the floorboard's chipped edges.

She sighed, pushing her hands through her hair, her eyes closing. She'd managed so long without drama, without anyone messing with her, without anyone guessing who and what she was. In the span of a few minutes, her life had gone from easy and boring, just as she liked it, to precarious and scary. Not only did she have a demon working her front door, but a witch had rifled through her things and destroyed her precious mirror, for her, a priceless artifact of her former life. Her jewels were the only other tangible remembrance of those years as Louis's mistress and friend, and she hadn't a clue where they were.

It seemed rather obvious to her that the witch had been there searching for the opal. What else would she want with Antoinette but that singular stone, imbued with such magic? The rest of the jewels were non-magical, beautiful remnants of a time long past. Antoinette wanted them all, but she especially wanted that opal. Maybe it was time she stepped up her efforts and started giving her all to the search. She'd become a little careless, believing the jewels would turn up eventually.

Before she could think much more about where to resume the hunt for her missing jewels, her cell phone rang.

It was Mark, her bouncer. She answered. "Mark, were you able to work things out with the sitter?" Antoinette knew there was an edge of hopeful desperation in her voice.

Mark cleared his throat on the other end. This was Mark's tell. Whenever he had bad news to impart, he cleared his throat first. "I'm really sorry, boss. The girl you sent me, although she seemed great at first, is now saying she needs to spend more time with her boyfriend and won't be able to help me any longer."

"Oh." Antoinette sighed. "Well, we'll just find someone else. I think Nicole said that her cousin is a college kid looking for evening work."

Mark cleared his throat again. More bad news was coming. "Like I said, boss, I'm really sorry, but I can't keep doing this to Abby. She's had to get used to so many sitters, and, really, I'm the one who should be home with her at night, making dinner and helping with homework. I can't tell you how much I've enjoyed working for you. You're truly the greatest boss I've ever had, but I'm going to have to move on. I've been offered a construction job. Not ideal, but the pay is good, and I'll be able to drop off Abby and pick her up after school. It's what's best for us, for now."

Antoinette closed her eyes, massaging her neck. "Of course, Mark. You have to do what's best for your family. I understand that." Antoinette didn't have family, didn't have anyone but herself, but still, she was sympathetic. "Please know that my door is always open to you should you need work, and please don't be a stranger."

"I appreciate that, boss. If it wasn't for you, hiring me when you did, I would have lost Abby. I'll never forget that, or you."

Antoinette ended the call. For the first time in a century, she felt close to tears. The back of her throat was so tight, she had to bite her lip to keep the tears from falling. Part of this was due to missing a great employee and part was self-pity. There was so much going on and now she'd have to find someone to fill an immediate opening. She was tired and had been more and more of late.

The *Employees Only* door opened and closed with a soft click, music from the club spilling down the hallway for only a second.

Deena popped her head around the corner. "Hey, just checking on you. Everything okay back here?"

Antoinette shrugged a shoulder, her eyes cloudy.

"Uh-oh." Deena entered the room, tiptoeing around the few remaining glass shards "Now what? Need some help with all this?"

Antoinette shook her head, clearing her throat as Mark had done. "Mark's not coming back."

"Shit," Deena said, leaning a hip against Antoinette's desk and sucking her bottom lip into her mouth as she stared at the ground. "Want me to start asking around, or do you want to talk to the brick wall out there?"

"The demon?"

"Huh?" Deena looked at her like she was crazy, then laughed. "Yeah, I guess he's fairly demonic. At least he was earlier, but you should see him handling the door. The man's a natural."

Antoinette laughed like what she'd said had been a joke. *Stupid, stupid.*

She'd blundered for the first time in her very long life. She must be tired. Never before had she unintentionally let something slip. Her words were always carefully chosen, had always been carefully chosen. She'd learned to think before she spoke as a mortal. One couldn't be complacent at court. That carefulness had also worked well for her as an immortal.

How could I have said something so thoughtless?

The best thing to do now would be to move on from the comment before Deena could make any associations. Deena was smart.

"I don't think Khaos is the right sort of element. I'm not sure he'll fit in with us."

Deena shrugged and made a face like she was thinking through what Antoinette had said. "Maybe. Or he might fit in perfectly. I'm not saying I like the man, but there's something about him that makes me think I could get to like him. Why don't we give him a trial? I mean, we need someone now. All hell will break loose without a strong man. Especially after what happened in here tonight."

Antoinette scowled as she looked around the trashed room. "A trial. A short trial of one week. If he displeases me once in that week, then he's out."

"Displeases." Deena laughed. "You have such a funny way of talking sometimes."

Antoinette shifted uncomfortably. "I told you I went to finishing school when I was young. My grandmother was a stickler for formality."

Deena laughed again. "I wonder how I'd do in finishing school." She pushed herself off the desk. "Okay, I'll go tell tall, dark, and demonic that if he wants the job, he's got a week to prove himself."

Tall, dark, and demonic.

"Wonderful," Antoinette muttered. She would now have to somehow keep Khaos at arm's length, while also searching for her jewels. One thing she didn't need was a demon breathing down her neck. Apparently, there was a witch already doing that.

Antoinette dropped into her office chair, her head lolling against the back. She stared up at the ceiling while she thought about her jewels. She had alerts set up to email her should anyone post about them online. There hadn't been a single alert since she'd done that. She regularly trolled the big auction houses and even had an online contact, a man she'd never met, who had made inquiries on her anonymous behalf at black markets all over the world. The jewels were in the wind. Unless they weren't.

The last time she'd seen them, they were at his home.

The Comte St. Germain, or Jacque, as she knew him, kept a house on Royal Street. A house that still stood, taunting her every day. The house was the most photographed in all of the French Quarter. The large brick building with the red door that opens onto the corner of Ursuline and Royal was probably so famous that even those who had never been to New Orleans would find it familiar. Antoinette hadn't stepped a single foot inside since her escape from Jacque, one that took her three months to plan.

Jacque hadn't known the secret of the opal. To him, the jewels were merely what they were—priceless gems fit for a queen, which Antoinette had nearly been. The gold casket, filigree around the edges, had been removed from her room to his. He sat the casket on his bedside table, knowing that she'd never be brave enough to go anywhere near his bed, not when he revolted her so. When the door was open, she could see the golden box, taunting her with its nearness, but she never stepped inside his room. Even on that last evening, the evening she knew would finally see her free of him, she didn't dare. The act would have given her away, and after all she'd been through, after all the planning, she couldn't let the pull of her jewels keep her from escaping. She'd had all she would need to get her back to France. Nothing else mattered.

She'd always thought that someone else, someone involved in that night, must have gotten their hands on those jewels, but they'd never turned up, so it stood to reason that the Comte had had the foresight to hide them that night before all hell had broken loose.

The only way to find out for sure if the jewels were still on the property was to go and look for herself. The one hitch in that plan was the fact that the house was still a single-family residence. Someone, or multiple people, still lived in that home on Royal Street. This would complicate her search, but nothing was impossible. She'd escaped when she'd thought she would die there, and now, she would get back in.

Royal Street was just getting busy at ten the next evening. The summer night was warm, the humidity from the day all but gone. Overhead, the skies were clear, the stars bright. On the street, gas lamps flickered, casting shadows around corners and down alleyways. Antoinette could smell the soft fumes.

The Comte's former home stood tall in front of her, the balconies sagging a bit. Most of the balconies in the French Quarter sagged. Often, Antoinette would walk beneath them, wondering when the inevitable collapse would come. She hoped the sidewalks underneath would be free of humans when they did come crashing down.

Sirens sounded in the distance, prompting Antoinette to dash down the alley to the courtyard behind her target, then scale the back wall like a superhero. There was no one about to witness her feat. Her senses would tell her if she were being watched.

She alighted onto the balcony of the room that once belonged to the Comte St. Germain and waited. On the opposite side of the glass door, she could hear the rhythmic breathing of the occupants. The room was dark, with a curtain drawn. Thankfully, it seemed that the couple inside went to bed early.

Red and blue flashing lights flooded the alley, bathing the courtyard's edges beneath her in ethereal light, but she was inside before anyone below could see her.

She wrapped her hand around the doorknob, breaking it and the lock in one single motion. With that, she was inside the room.

There wasn't much time to dawdle, so she laid a hand on the gentleman's shoulder. He startled awake, but the intensity of her eyes held him in place. "You're about to enter the deepest sleep of your life. You won't wake no matter what you hear or how bright the light is." His eyes closed, and she rushed to the other side of the bed to give the woman the same instructions.

With the house to herself, she began her search of the Comte's old rooms. She did her best to ignore the old feelings washing over her.

What she saw was this—other than the modern furniture, the room hadn't changed. The fireplace, surrounded by rust-red tile and topped with a carved oak mantle, was still the same. The mouth was charred around the edges, the smell of soot strong in the air as it had always been. As Antoinette drew closer, she noticed the two red tiles near the bottom on the right were still cracked, the victims of one of the Comte's late-night temper tantrums. She ran a hand along the smooth mantle and looked around. The oak floors hadn't been replaced or covered with tacky carpet, and the walls were still textured like whipped meringue. The bed, no longer the luxurious four-poster but now a squat sort of thing without a headboard, sat in the same place the Comte's dramatic bed had, centered between the two verandah doors.

Images assaulted her as she took stock of the room. She saw her and the Comte in a heated argument near the fireplace; she saw her and the Comte laughing at some drunken passersby under the verandah window; she saw herself walking by the open door on her last night in the cursed home, one eye on her jewel casket as it sat by his bed. Her feelings for the Comte had been confused at first; they shared a few laughs and a few good times, but his constant need to have control over every aspect of her life, ultimately not even letting her leave, was what ruined their complicated friendship. Add to that his depravity. Along with these images, she also saw the girls he tortured tied to chairs in the corner, their lifeblood dripping away. The Comte was many things, but above all, he was a monster first.

Shaking these thoughts from her head, she got down to business. Standing about moping over the past would not serve her. She had a mission. She was in that place for a reason.

Had he hidden the jewels, they would not be out in the open. The first place Antoinette searched was the fireplace. She pressed every tile, hoping for a secret compartment, but none sprang forth. She leaned inside the sooty mouth and felt as high up as her arms would allow. There were no secret apertures.

Ignoring the soot covering her arms, she felt along the walls, knocking here and there to see if there were hidden hollow spaces. The vents were all empty. Floorboards were pried up to the same effect. The room held no secrets. She went to the next room, searching each in turn with vampiric speed.

In fifteen minutes, she'd searched every nook and cranny of the Comte's former home from top to bottom.

The disappointment was nearly overwhelming. Antoinette collapsed against a hallway wall, raking her still-dirty hands through her hair. If the jewels weren't there, then where could they be? The Comte's home was the last place she'd seen them. There was nowhere else she could think of. Her heart began to race, her thoughts a tumble in her mind.

She closed her eyes, took a deep breath, and thought back to that night.

As soon as she'd woken, she'd decided the time of her escape had come. She'd dashed off a quick letter to the authorities, detailing that the Comte St. Germain had returned to New Orleans and was living within the walls of his old residence. After they'd run him out of town the last time, the authorities would certainly want to investigate. What a ghastly scene that had been. A tortured young woman had escaped her bonds and leaped from the balcony. She'd later died, but before her death, she told the police all about the Comte's house of horrors. If everything went to plan, the police would come and come quickly. Getting their hands on him a second time would be a big win for their little department.

Antoinette had gone to her balcony, knowing the Comte, a late sleeper, was still stirring in his room. When a young boy had walked by, Antoinette tossed the letter along with a good bit of coin and said one word: police.

The boy nodded and ran off. For the next hour, Antoinette paced about her room. The Comte had knocked on her door to invite her down to the parlor for a bite of the woman he'd taken the day before, but she'd refused. He'd gotten used to her melancholy, so he stalked away without another word.

A satchel was packed with all the things she'd need to get home to France. It waited, stuffed under her bed.

Not prone to nerves, Antoinette chewed her nails incessantly, listening for any sound that would herald the arrival of the police. None came. Not for a full two hours. Antoinette had begun to lose hope, to believe that the boy had taken her money and thrown away the letter. But just as she was about to give up on the whole affair, she'd heard a soft rustle below her window followed by the muffled voices of several men.

It was then that Antoinette left her room. She could hear the Comte and the poor woman he'd stolen off the streets, whimpering in pain. The policemen entered the home abruptly and with much fanfare as they rammed the door open below. That was when Antoinette spied her casket. She was about to dash for her precious jewels when the thudding of rubber boots thundered up the stairs.

She didn't have time for the jewels. It wouldn't take the police long to realize she was a vampire, too. The Comte would surely give her away. He'd never done anything to protect her before, why would he then? A handful of humans she could have dealt with, but thirty? She'd been too young in the blood then.

So, she'd left them. It was either the jewels or her life, and she'd chosen her life. The life she'd found back in France wasn't much of one, but it was far better than the tortuous existence she'd lived with the Comte. At least in

France, she'd been free.

She couldn't see how the Comte had had time to move the jewels, so it stood to reason that they'd been taken by someone else. Perhaps one of the officers who'd detained the Comte that night had stolen them. Possibly, those men had divided the bounty among themselves, and the collection was no longer intact. The fact was that so many years had passed since that night that finding the jewels, particularly the opal, seemed impossible.

Antoinette was tired. Tired from a long immortal life that had never been fully realized. Of course, nothing could compare to her human life, so she longed to be mortal again. Not only had she been someone, but she'd stood for something. All she'd done as an immortal was hide.

There wasn't time to dwell. Based on the groans she could hear, one or more of the family members was stirring.

Antoinette said her last goodbye to the house on Royal. Before she jumped from the verandah to the courtyard down below, she did something very unlike her, she extended her middle finger to the Comte's old room. "Goodbye, you old bastard," she whispered before she stepped up onto the wrought iron railing.

The second the balls of her feet hit the stone below, the fine hairs on the back of her neck raised. She wasn't alone. Antoinette pressed herself against the cool exterior brick of the house as she let her preternatural eyes take in the shadows around her. There were no sounds other than the muffled voices coming from within and some sirens in the distance.

A branch moved a split second before a dark shape came out of a corner recess, pinning her where she stood with a strength that took her breath away. She tried to fight, tried to push back against the witch that had invaded her office, but her arms were held in a vise grip over her head.

She shouldn't be stronger than me.

"And why shouldn't I be?"

Antoinette stared at her, eyes wide. "You read my

thoughts."

"Obviously. You're not too bright, are you?"

Antoinette's chest and cheeks flushed red. She felt hot all over. All she wanted to do was blast this upstart into the stone wall of the courtyard behind, but still, Antoinette couldn't budge. So, instead of fighting, she stilled. She calmed her breath and willed her heartbeat into a steadier rhythm. While she did these things, she took stock of her enemy. The woman whose face was inches from her own was probably in her mid-thirties. There was a telltale creasing around the brown eyes that was fresh, the lines were new and not yet etched in deep. Her skin was what Antoinette would call olive, the hair long and white, held back in a tight ponytail. The witch was taller than Antoinette, which was not a difficult feat, as she was so slight, but this woman must have been nearly six feet tall, the same as Deena.

She stooped down to hover over Antoinette.

"What do you want from me?" Antoinette asked, wanting to fight but remaining calm. There was no point, so why waste the energy? Antoinette had an idea that this woman was after the same thing she was, but Antoinette knew when to play dumb.

The witch rolled her eyes. "I don't buy the stupid girl act. You know exactly what I'm after, that's why you came here. I need those jewels, Antoinette. But they weren't inside, were they? I thought maybe you'd hidden them here after the search of your office came up empty. But you don't know where they are, do you?"

"You thought I had the jewels?" Antoinette was annoyed. Her wrists were getting sore, and the position she was in was just downright humiliating. There was no point in playing dumb, just as there was no point in struggling. If the witch knew about the jewels, which she clearly did, only one person could have told her about them.

"They were last in your possession."

"That's where you're wrong." Antoinette wasn't saying

anything else. The time had come to extricate herself from this mess.

The witch cocked her head to the side. Antoinette had the impression she was trying to read her for some tell that she was lying, or perhaps she was trying to read her mind again. Antoinette wiped her mind of all thought, focusing on nothing but the pain in her wrists.

The witch's gaze raked her face, a quizzical expression etching a deep line between her brows. "I don't believe you," she said.

"Who are you?" Antoinette asked.

"You can call me Jadis." The witch scowled. "And that's all you'll get from me."

Enough was enough. Antoinette tried to keep her mind free while working out how to escape. Not an easy feat. A strategy wouldn't be helpful here, only brawn. Antoinette kept thinking of the pain in her arms, how they felt weak. As Jadis drew slightly back, Antoinette sprung. She kicked up a knee, hitting the witch hard between her legs. She may not have a penis, but Antoinette knew the kick would still hurt and throw her opponent off-kilter.

Jadis sucked in a breath, loosening her grip on Antoinette's wrists. That was all Antoinette needed to pull herself free. She took Jadis by her shoulders and shoved with all her might. The woman hit the stone wall of the courtyard with a loud, crunching thud. Something broke, probably ribs. Antoinette didn't need to stick around to find out whatever it was. She should have finished the witch off, but she didn't know what Jadis was capable of. Antoinette had already been taken by surprise.

She turned on her heel to run out of the open courtyard gate, but before she could get farther than two feet away, Jadis was on her back, shoving her onto the hard ground. Antoinette's elbows bit cobblestone, her flesh peeling away as she slid.

Rather than turning onto her back, Jadis was too strong for a head-to-head fight, Antoinette mustered every preternatural bone in her body to get to her knees and buck the witch off. Jadis flew backward, again hitting something behind them with another sickening crunch. This time, Antoinette heard her choking for breath. At the least, the witch had had the wind knocked from her, at the most she'd broken more bones. Without looking back, Antoinette sped out of the courtyard and down the alley.

Running home with preternatural speed, Antoinette kept to alleys and shadows lest a human spy her flying by. All she wanted was to be back safe in her little refuge. But was she safe there? It no longer appeared that way.

AD BRAZEAU

CHAPTER EIGHT

Khaos arrived early for his shift. He aimed to talk to Antoinette to make sure the witch hadn't made a return. Getting to know Antoinette better in the process wouldn't hurt either. Khaos often found women attractive, but there was something about this particular woman that was causing him to feel in ways he didn't think possible. He'd been excited to head to Noir. He couldn't have imagined ever feeling excitement over punching a clock, but his heart had skipped a beat as he pulled into the parking lot. He knew quite well it wasn't the job. It was her.

He'd spent the night in a motel room on the outskirts of the Quarter. The accommodations hadn't been the luxury he was used to, but the bed and the bathroom had been clean. He'd used the hundred dollars he'd gotten in tips from the night before, having yet to touch the last vestiges of cash he'd had on him when he'd left his parents' house. Since he didn't have to eat food, at least he wouldn't have to pay for that, but there would be other expenses soon. He'd need gas for his Lambo, which only took premium, and he'd have to pay for the insurance at the beginning of the month. Insuring a Lamborghini was not cheap. Parked behind the motel for the evening, the car had caused quite a stir among the residents, who appeared to Khaos to be mostly ladies of the night. He'd kept one eye on the car until dawn, stirring anytime he'd heard so much as a peep outside the room's window.

He may have to make a hard decision about his baby sooner rather than later. Lucky for him, there was a small lot behind Noir designated *Employee Parking*. At least the car would be relatively safe while he worked.

While walking into the bar through the back door, an ache pulsed in Khaos's loins. He'd spent last night without the company of a woman. He wasn't sure why he hadn't. Attracted to Antoinette, or not, there had been ample opportunity, as there always was. Last night, the goth beauties who'd offered themselves up on silver platters totaled double digits. Khaos told himself he was merely tired, that yesterday had been hard. There needn't be any more explanation than that.

Khaos took in the atmosphere of the bar before walking in further. The place was filling up. He needed to take up his post but wanted to see Antoinette first.

The lovely Nicole, in a vintage dress with white sneakers, was wiping down the bar when Khaos slunk up, leaning against the dark wood.

"Is Antoinette in the back?" he asked. He thought asking before barging his way into her office was in his best interest.

Nicole shook her brown curls. "Nope. Oddly, she went out this evening. If you need something you can ask Deena."

Khaos glanced over his shoulder to see Deena moving from table to table, lighting the cut glass votives. He returned his attention to Nicole. "What do you mean, *oddly.*"

Nicole shrugged. "The boss never leaves the back rooms. Like ever." She turned her back on him to straighten the bottles along the mirrored wall.

Khaos thought it was funny that everyone in

Antoinette's employ called her *the boss*. For such a small woman, who never left her office, she certainly commanded a lot of respect.

Just as he was about to request a glass of water, they definitely wouldn't allow him to drink alcohol, there was a sound in the back. Someone entered, followed by a scuffling and a huff as a door was slammed, a deadbolt sliding home.

With Nicole's and Deena's attention elsewhere, Khaos slid off the barstool and made for the *Employees Only* entrance that led to Antoinette. No one stopped him.

Khaos took two massive strides until he stood in the doorway of Antoinette's office. There she was, slumped in a chair, massaging her left shoulder. She stopped as soon as she saw him, her arms dropping to her lap, her face placid even though a bruise was visible under her right eye. Khaos knew when someone was trying to affect an air of nonchalance. He wasn't buying it.

"What happened to you?" He moved to the opposite chair, standing behind it, his hands on the headrest.

"Nothing. I've been cleaning up the mess from last night." She looked straight at him, her brow smooth, her mouth a flat line. This was a woman used to subterfuge. Khaos had to remind himself that she was no doubt adept at playing and winning games as she was once a powerful figure in a powerful court.

The office had been cleaned. That much was true. The glass had been cleared away, the furniture put right. The only tell that something was amiss was the faint outline on the tan-colored wall where the ornate mirror had once hung.

Khaos sighed, rolling his eyes. "I thought we were beyond the fabrications, Antoinette. I know you've been out. Not only did I hear you come in and throw the deadbolt as if you were in fear of being chased, but you have a bruise on your face, the sleeve of your jacket is torn, and your hair looks like it's been through a tornado." He crossed his arms. "You've been in a scuffle. I'd like to know who with."

Antoinette scowled, fingered the tear in her jacket, then

leaned forward to pull it off. "I don't owe you any sort of explanation, demon. We're not friends. You are my employee, and that is all."

Khaos narrowed his eyes, arms still crossed. He was unfazed by her remark. "It was that witch, wasn't it? The one from last night? According to your other employees, you never leave these rooms, so what else could draw you outdoors?"

Antoinette flung the torn jacket on the floor with a grunt. She crossed her arms now, throwing herself back against the chair. Her eyes were a storm as she stared at him. "I don't need your help."

Khaos did his level best not to quirk a smile. "As you've said. However, you have a demon in your possession, Madame, so why not use me?"

Antoinette raked his face with her gaze.

Khaos felt his blood quicken and his body warm as she appraised him. This woman was not his usual type. She was tiny, like a bird. She'd be frail if she were human. She wore no makeup, no ornamentation of any kind. Her style was simple, unadorned. The kind he usually went for was curvaceous, flesh bursting out of their lycra mini dresses. And yet, he was drawn to her. Whether it was because of her historical past, or something in her character, he couldn't help but admit that he was attracted. Antoinette was interesting, there was no denying that.

After a few seconds, her shoulders relaxed against the back of the chair. "I suppose you're right. I've exhausted the one possibility and have no idea where to look next."

Khaos moved around the chair opposite Antoinette. He plopped down. "First, why don't you let me heal you, then I need to know a little more about what it is we're looking for."

Antoinette's mouth screwed up as she stared off at the cold fireplace. "What do you mean *heal me*? I'm a vampire, my bruises will heal on their own by tomorrow night." She continued massaging her shoulder.

Khaos tried not to look too smoldering. He knew Antoinette's vampire blood would heal her without any problems, but the old devil still lurked within. He wanted the opportunity to get close to her, to hold her in his arms, touch her skin, flesh that looked as smooth as marble, if only for a moment.

"I'm aware of how quickly you'll heal through your own powers," he started. "But I can heal you like that." He snapped his fingers. "I can take away your discomfort in a second. Faster than a second."

She narrowed her eyes, the skepticism obvious in her wrinkled brow. "How?"

"With my blood, of course. Demon blood is holier than the sacrament."

Antoinette's eyes went wide and from her burst forth one quick laugh. "I don't know if I'd use the word *holy* to describe anything demonic."

Khaos shrugged, amused by her amusement. "One drop of my blood will take away every pain in your body. Demon blood is a thousand times more healing than vampire blood." He left out the other part. The part about how his blood produced a pleasurable effect that was very nearly orgasmic. He knew this was wicked on his part and borderline wrong, but he was still himself, after all.

She continued to stare at him with her eyes narrowed. When her shoulder, the healthy one, relaxed by a degree, he knew he had her. "One drop?"

"One drop."

"Fine. I want to be able to sleep later and I'm pretty sure my shoulder is dislocated, if not broken."

"Easy," he said, moving forward in the chair, his voice dropping an octave. "How would you like it?"

Antoinette rolled her eyes. "Just give me your wrist."

"Done." Khaos rolled up the sleeve of his white shirt, then stretched out his arm.

Antoinette grasped his forearm with a grip that surprised him. She was strong. Even injured, this was no weak human woman. He had to stop himself from growling at the thought.

Antoinette bent over him. She opened her mouth, her fangs lengthening, then bit into his arm as if it were an apple.

Khaos sucked in a breath. The act was also pleasurable for him, another tidbit he'd kept to himself. He laid a hand on the back of her neck as she drank. She had the neck of a swan—long, graceful. He closed his eyes as a wave of pleasure passed through him but did his best not to make it known. This wasn't his first rodeo.

When she released him, he opened his eyes to watch her, her mouth still agape, a trickle of his blood at the corner of her mouth. She was panting as she collapsed into her chair. A shudder rocked her body, causing Khaos to grin like the devil he was. "Was it good for you?"

"You knew that would happen," she panted, wiping the corner of her mouth. Still, her face was soft as she gazed at him.

"It's the same with vampires, isn't it?" He shrugged as he leaned back.

"Not quite. I'd be angry if I didn't feel so good."

Now it was Khaos's turn to be shocked. He stared at her with wide eyes.

"Not like that." She shook her head, rolling her eyes. "I mean physically."

Khaos's eyebrows lifted higher. "That's what I thought you meant."

"No, I meant my injuries. You were right, every pain released the second your blood hit my system."

Khaos offered what he knew was his most devastating grin. "Well, Madame, if you're ever in need of another blood offering, I'm at service."

She rolled her eyes again, a hard sigh escaping her lips. "You're exasperating."

"Yes, I know. You'll be a champion eye-roller before you know it. Now, it's time to move on, I think. Tell me more about what happened. I have to know what we're looking for, Antoinette. I can't help you otherwise."

She sighed. "My jewels."

Khaos's brow wrinkled. He'd expected something a little more interesting than jewels. Perhaps something magical or paranormal. Why was a witch interested in run-of-the-mill gems?

"These jewels must be something else."

"They are." Antoinette continued staring into the fireplace. "The casket of jewels taken from me is priceless in today's market. Two years ago, two of Marie Antoinette's diamond bracelets sold at auction for over eight million dollars. That was just for two pieces of jewelry. My casket contained over thirty. There was a diamond necklace with a center stone of forty carats. That's one piece. Everything in that collection was designed for me by Louis. He chose every stone. Imagine what that collection, the collection of the famed Madame de Pompadour, would be worth at Sotheby's today. A hundred million might be a good starting point."

"Okay." Khaos crossed his feet at the ankles. "I can see why someone would want to get their hands on these jewels. But wouldn't a witch use a locator spell and be done?"

Antoinette shrugged. "Not if the jewels were spelled before they were hidden."

"Right. And how would this witch even know about the jewels? Are they known? For example, Marie Antoinette was painted wearing some of her pieces in portraits. Was it the same for you?"

"Some of my jewels were worn in portraits, yes."

"Okay," Khaos said again. He was trying to read Antoinette, which was hard. There wasn't anything about her current demeanor that suggested she was lying, but Khaos had known some good liars in his day. He was a grand champion of the fib. If she wasn't lying, she had to be at least holding something back. He still couldn't quite wrap his head around how a witch would know anything about her jewels, or her, unless the witch was also some sort of historian or treasure hunter. This brought up a good question. "How does the witch know about you? I thought you were a hermit who never left Noir."

She glanced at him then, her brows knit together. "You're right. How does she know about me? I rarely leave. I don't like the word *hermit*, but that's probably how my staff would describe me. I only go out when I absolutely need sustenance, then I come right back."

"Where did you go tonight?"

Antoinette looked back toward the fireplace. Eye contact was not her thing.

"I went to the old home of the Comte St. Germain."

"St. Germain. I've heard of him. Wasn't he a famous New Orleans vampire?"

Antoinette rolled her eyes, but only slightly. She'd probably never rolled her eyes so many times in a row. "I suppose he was famous in his own right. He's known for showing up throughout time, having never aged. In New Orleans, he lived on Royal Street where he gave elaborate parties but never drank or ate. Long ago, a woman he was feeding from escaped him by jumping over the railing of the home. She ended up dying, the house was searched, and Germain had vanished. Years later, he returned with me in tow. I also wanted to escape Germain, so I alerted the authorities to his return. They stormed the house. That was the last time I saw him and my casket of jewels."

"Wait." Khaos held up a hand. "Are you telling me that the Comte St. Germain is your maker?" A famous woman sired by a famous vampire. Khaos had thought he'd heard everything.

"That is what I'm telling you. He came to the court of Versailles during my thirty-eighth year. He became rather enamored of me, but I didn't like him. I did my best to avoid him, but this was hard, as he seemed to be around every corner I turned. One evening, after I'd left Louis's apartment, I came upon him skulking in a dark hall with a Duchess. He invited me to his rooms for a parting drink.

He said he was leaving Versailles and had invited a few people to his rooms to say goodbye. I was wary, but as I knew the Duchess, I felt it was safe to have this one drink and then never have to see him again. The moment I entered his room, I was uneasy. It was just the three of us, and the Duchess didn't seem herself. She was in a daze. I later realized she'd been mesmerized and was only there to lure me in. The Comte poured a thick red liquid into each of our glasses. He said it was a new type of Italian wine, and, indeed, it smelled like red wine, but also something else. We drank. I nearly spat out the liquid, but my breeding wouldn't allow for anything so unbecoming, so I swallowed. What happened next was all darkness. When I woke, lying on the floor, I was not the same. He was sitting in a chair, his legs crossed, staring smugly down at me. It was then he'd told me what he'd done, and what I'd become. I screamed for the guard. He was thrown out of Versailles, laughing all the while. As the guards were pulling him out of his rooms, he yelled to me that when they found out, and they would, I could find him in New Orleans."

Khaos leaned forward. "And did they find out?"

"Louis was the one who figured it out in the end. I'd managed to mostly fool the court for four years. It was easy to feign illness in those days. I slept during the day and kept mostly to myself, meeting with Louis in the evenings. By then, Louis and I were no longer lovers. We were friends, and I retained my status in the court by being an advisor to him. This was unheard of, but I had the respect of everyone, including the Queen, who was my friend. One night, during what would have been my forty-second year, Louis looked at me, and said, 'You know, my love, they won't believe it for much longer.' Somehow, he knew. We devised a plan, Louis and I, that included a faked death and a midnight escape. Louis put me on a boat for the colonies with my jewels and a large purse of money. My time at Versailles had come to an end. When I arrived in Charleston, I made my way to New Orleans, almost like I was on some sort of autopilot. I didn't want to go to the Comte, but I also didn't know how to make my way alone in a foreign place."

"I'm amazed how you survived at Versailles for four years. How did you feed? How did you control the thirst as a newly made vampire?"

Antionette shrugged again. "Control is in my DNA. As a woman who'd risen to such heights on her wits and intelligence, I wasn't going to let my baser instincts take over. I learned early how to take small drinks from servants and courtiers. The wounds would heal instantly, and I could mesmerize my victims into thinking they were tired. Believe me, it was hard. I remember the first time like it was yesterday. The first victim was my ladies' maid. How I wanted to rip out her whole throat and feast on the sweet blood. But I made myself feel her heartbeat. I made myself say her name over and over in my mind as I drank. When I'd had enough to sustain me, probably a little too much that first time, I forced myself to pull away. I was still so very thirsty, but I stopped. I laid her little body down on the marble floor. The wound in her neck was grievous, the blood still flowing. Somehow, I knew, an instinct, I suppose, to prick my finger and smear my blood over the gash. I was giddy when it healed. Like an animal, I licked up the spilled blood. Then I looked into her eyes, another instinct, and told her she was feeling unwell and to go to bed, that she would be fine in the morning. When she came to me the next day, a little tired but none the worse for wear, I knew I could make it work, at least for a time."

"That's incredible, Antoinette, truly." Khaos shook his head. "From what I've been told, the first few weeks of a new vampire's existence are tortuous, the thirst unforgiving."

"It is. For me, the transition was no less tortuous. The difference was that I had crafted my existence down to the last detail. Everything about me, about my life, was orchestrated, by me. I was not for one second going to let anything derail what I'd built. Not until I was ready. When

Louis showed his cards, I knew the time had come, but again, I had control of the plan, the death, and the escape."

Khaos wasn't usually impressed by people outside of his circle, but he was impressed now. Antoinette's story made him want to help her even more. No, she wasn't looking for anything mystical, her jewels were just jewels, but they were *her* jewels, remnants of a life that had meant so much to her.

"So, you went to the Comte's house to look for the jewels because the night the police came for him was the last time you saw him?"

"Yes."

"But you didn't find them?"

"No."

"Why hadn't you gone there to look before?"

"The honest answer to that is I don't know. I guess I thought the jewels would eventually show up at auction somewhere. I could hire someone to steal them back for me, one by one, and all would be well. But they've never shown up anywhere. There was a small chance the Comte had stashed them somewhere in the house, but I'm sure now that they're not there."

"And you have no idea where to look next?"

Antoinette shook her head.

"There's only one way I can see forward, and that's with magic. Spelled or not, I want to talk to my aunt and uncle. They're both powerful witches out in the bayou. Even if they can't help, they seem like our best option."

"How are they our best option if they can't help?"

"My hope is they can at least nudge us in the right direction. But you're not the only one with instincts. If my instincts are sound, Fosette and Lucian should have an answer."

"The other witch can't seem to find the answer." Antoinette didn't seem convinced. "Her name is Jadis, by the way. At least I learned something."

"Fosette and Lucian aren't your everyday witches. Their power is strong, old, and unique. I'm asking you to trust me."

Antoinette studied him once again. "All right. I don't have a lot of options, so if you think you can get me some answers, I trust that. Anyway, what do I have to lose?"

Khaos grinned. "Nothing you haven't lost before."

CHAPTER NINE

A horn blaring outside woke her up. The room, her bedroom, was bathed in darkness. With her vampiric eyes, Antoinette could see everything as she reposed in her four-poster bed, the chenille coverlet pulled up to her chin. Her room was styled in much the same way her bedroom at Versailles had been, only the dimensions were not quite so grand. She'd hung the chinoiserie wallpaper herself, delighting in the silver-foiled design of cranes standing in water. The two chests were mismatched antiques she'd found online several years ago. Noir had been doing well, but not that well, so she purchased the dressers and the bed second-hand and refinished them herself.

The chandelier was new, a Christmas gift to herself last year after the fantastic year-to-date returns from her business.

Her home on the second floor was a cozy one. The apartment consisted of three bedrooms, two bathrooms, a living room, and a kitchen. Of course, the kitchen was never used, but to keep up appearances, as she did have her employees upstairs on occasion, the room was outfitted with dishes, pots, pans, and everything else she needed to appear like a normal human. The kitchen was what modern-day people called eat-in, with a small table and chairs in the corner that were never used.

She threw back the coverlet and rolled from the bed. Her usual routine was to open the velvet curtains wide and peer out on the scene below. Her window opened to Chartres Street, the front door to her bar just underneath her bedroom. But tonight, she was going to ready herself for an unusual adventure. She was going to leave her domicile for the second night in a row, and she could hardly believe where she was going. Deena would never believe it, which is why Antoinette had told her the previous evening that she was leaving on an overnight to Baton Rouge to source new seating for the bar. The bar didn't need new seating, which Deena pointed out, but Antoinette had merely smiled, and said, "*I'm thinking of changing a few things up.*"

Had Deena looked at her as if she'd lost her mind? Absolutely. But her manager hadn't argued further. Not until Antoinette told her that Khaos would be accompanying her.

"*Have you lost it?*" Deena had blurted. "*You're going on a trip with that guy? And who's going to work the door?*"

Deena hadn't offered any apology for the outburst as she stared at Antoinette.

Antoinette knew the questions were valid, that Deena was worried about her being alone with Khaos, a man they hardly knew. Deena wasn't aware her boss was a vampire who could take care of herself.

"*I understand why you're concerned,*" she had said. "*But I need the muscle if I decide to make any purchases. We have separate hotel rooms. As for who is working the door tonight, I managed to get Mark to come for a one-night-only gig. I offered him a special rate, which with his daughter's birthday coming up, he readily accepted. So, we're covered.*"

That seemed to placate Deena. A little.

Now, it was time for Antoinette to get herself ready for the real excursion—a trip to the bayou.

She'd been, and remained, pessimistic, about the whole affair. Outside of the witch she'd tangled with in the search for her jewels, she'd never known a witch. She knew they were out there, but the solitary life she lived generally kept her shielded from such things.

Khaos had sung the praises of his witches, Fosette and Lucian, endlessly the night before, but that didn't mean much to Antoinette. She trusted Khaos about as far as she could throw him. He'd withheld rather vital information from her. He'd known, one hundred percent, what his blood would do to her and how it would make her feel. But he'd kept that tidbit to himself. If she were human, she'd accuse him of sexual misconduct. Yes, he had her consent for the blood exchange, but she'd consented without all the information. If she didn't need him to help her find the jewels, he would have found himself out on his ear.

As it was, she did need him, and she knew it. As a demon, Khaos had powers she did not have, and his family seemed full of powerful beings. Having them on her side would be helpful. So, for now, she would put up with his immature antics, making sure she was always on her guard. If there was one thing Antoinette knew how to deal with, it was men who thought they were smarter than her.

She slipped out of her blush pink nightgown, tossing it in the hamper and pulling out a pair of jeans from her tall chest. She put these on, then pulled a black sweater from inside her closet. Next to go on was a pair of black lace-up boots over a thick pair of socks. When Antoinette thought of the bayou, a place she hadn't been to for over fifty years, she thought of dampness and dirt.

Inside a brown leather satchel went another pair of jeans and a sweater, this one tan, and a clean pair of underwear. As a vampire, she didn't have to worry too much about cleanliness, but she did like fresh clothes, and she bathed every day even though she could have never washed again and would remain as fresh as the day she was turned. Bathing was a luxury and a habit she could not do without.

She shouldered the satchel, locked her front door, and headed downstairs to the alley where Khaos would be waiting.

Avoiding any more run-ins with Deena was simple as the back stairs were private to her apartment, spilling out at the end of the hall opposite the employee entrance into Noir proper. Her office was along the hallway, as was the staff bathroom.

It felt odd to her to be turning left to the exterior door instead of to the right toward her office, but that's exactly what she did. The door, a heavy stainless steel, was chained, bolted, and alarmed. They'd never had a break-in until the witch.

Antoinette undid the chain, slid back the bolt, and punched in her code for the alarm. This is how the door would remain until Deena resecured it for the night at closing time. Employees, who parked in the alley, entered through the small courtyard gate with a four-digit code and accessed the door with a key, as it automatically locked from the outside.

Antoinette stepped into the courtyard, the bright light from the streetlight she'd had installed shining down on her like a spotlight. Antoinette was a stickler for safety.

There, outside the courtyard gate, idling in an employee parking spot, was a slick, expensive-looking car Antoinette couldn't have identified if someone had paid her. The driver's side window rolled down, and an arm, thick and tattooed, belonging to the one and only Khaos, beckoned her forward.

This felt dramatic. Antoinette couldn't help but roll her eyes as she rushed to the passenger door.

"Expensive car for a bouncer," she said as she slipped into the buttery leather seat. She may not have known what the car was, but she knew expensive when she saw it.

"Yeah, I may not have it for much longer." The playful tone usually prevalent in Khaos's voice was nonexistent.

"Why? Can't afford the payments?" The comment was

unkind and unlike Antoinette, but she wanted to punish him for last night.

"There are no payments, but yeah, something like that." He reversed out of the small lot.

As the car moved forward out of the alley, Antoinette glanced at his profile. She realized she didn't know anything about this man other than that he was a demon with an aunt and uncle who were witches. Where he lived, what the rest of his family dynamic was like were mysteries to her. This seemed unbalanced, as she had bared her soul to him, telling him more than she'd ever told anyone about herself the night before.

He was focused on the road ahead, his gaze hard, his mouth set in a straight line. This was not the way to begin an adventure with someone.

"I'm sorry," she said as she watched him. "That was mean and not at all like me. I'm sorry you may have to give up your car."

Khaos shrugged a massive shoulder. "It's a car. I'm coming to realize that things like that might not be such a big deal after all."

Antoinette nodded, although he couldn't see her. "There are many more important things in life, for sure. What's prompted the epiphany, if I may ask?"

Khaos looked away as he checked oncoming traffic before turning onto Canal Street. "I don't care to talk about it."

Antoinette scoffed at the rebuff, settling herself more comfortably in her seat for the long drive. "Seems fair. Especially since I told you my life's story."

He huffed a laugh, casting a sidelong look her way. "I guess I can't argue with that, but where to begin is the question."

Antoinette crossed her arms. "I always find the beginning a good place to start."

"The beginning is unremarkable. I was an orphaned demon adopted by two immortals, a prince of the

Underworld who was banished for snogging Persephone and cursed to live as a vampire-demon hybrid, and the daughter of Persephone, now an immortal herself."

"That's unremarkable?" Antoinette had nearly choked on her words as she interrupted. "How the hell is that unremarkable?"

Khaos shrugged again, but this time a smirk brightened his features. "For a demon, there isn't much that surprises you. Shall I continue?"

"After that tease, you better."

Khaos laughed. "Well, my parents, Theron and Greer, were great. My mom is gentle and kind, smart and resourceful. My dad ... well, my dad's a demon, so he's a little harder, a little gruffer, but has always been loving in his way. Little me, and now big me, tried their patience to no end, and a few days ago, my dad had had enough and kicked me out. Mom let him. My life was, how should I say it, privileged as all hell."

"Hence, the car."

"Exactly. The car, the house I lived in, clothes, money. I wanted for nothing."

"Why did they kick you out?"

"Too much hard partying."

"I see. Too much hard partying and not enough contribution?"

"Yeah, something like that." Khaos's eyes had gone hard again. "I've been shacking up in a motel on the outskirts of the Quarter. Let's just say that on the first day, I was disgusted by the humanity around me, but pretty quickly I began to see that those humans are just people trying to get by. Something about them has tugged at something deep inside me."

"A heart?"

Khaos looked to the side, so that, for a brief moment, Antoinette couldn't read his features. When he gazed back at the street, the set of his eyes looked sad to her.

"Sorry. I was mean again."

He shook his head. "No, you're right. There's a lady in the room next to mine. She's a prostitute with a little boy. His name is Henry and he's eight years old. When she has men over, Henry sits outside their room in a red plastic chair and reads a book with his headphones on. The sadness I felt seeing that little boy sit there while his mom does what she has to, it's touched me in a place I didn't know existed. I was thinking I could sell this car, probably make around three hundred thousand on it."

"Three hundred thousand? Dollars?" Antoinette screeched. She'd interrupted, but she couldn't help herself. Who in their right mind would pay so much for a car?

Khaos nodded. "Yeah. I never felt gross about it, but believe me, I'm starting to. Anyway, I thought I could sell it, find myself better accommodations, and maybe help out little Henry and his mom, too."

Antoinette was touched. Khaos was not as he'd seemed during that first encounter at Noir. That first night, he'd been drunken, disgusting, leering at women and making her employees and customers uncomfortable. But the same night, he'd come back to apologize, helped her out of a jam, was still helping her, and was talking about helping some woman with no ties to him simply because he felt for her son. There were layers to this man. Khaos hadn't gone into detail about what *hard partying* had meant, but Antoinette could guess. Sometimes all it took for someone to change was to upend their world. His parents had done that, and it seemed like their tough love was working.

"If you do decide to sell the car and can find Henry and his mom a better place to live, I'll give her a job. I pay well, very well, with benefits, and we can help her with childcare. I wish I had done a better job helping Mark with childcare, but it worked out and he has a better situation now. For this woman, I'll do more."

They pulled up to a stoplight, which allowed Khaos to look over at her, a half-smile pulling up one side of his face into the most attractive grin Antoinette had ever seen. His black eyes shined in the red light swinging above them, giving them a wicked glow. "I appreciate that. Know anyone who wants to buy a Lamborghini Aventador?"

"Is that what this is?" Antoinette ran her hands over the soft leather seats. "Not off the top of my head, but I'm sure we can find someone who wants to own a look-at-me car."

Khaos laughed. "Oh, yeah. I'll get it sold."

He revved the engine as the light turned green and sped off.

"Definitely hard to keep a low profile in this thing." She kind of enjoyed the speed, her stomach diving a bit as the car took off. She imagined the feeling must be akin to riding a roller coaster. "Now tell me more about these witches."

CHAPTER TEN

The cityscape of New Orleans flew past them as they drove through the night. Usually, Khaos enjoyed looking at the scene around him as he drove, taking in the beautiful architecture that made New Orleans famous. But tonight ... tonight was different. All he could focus on was the woman next to him. If he didn't know better, he'd think she'd bewitched him, cast a spell of lingering attraction. Because that was the thing, Khaos often found himself attracted to women, but not for long. Once he'd had them in his bed, the spell was broken. On many occasions, the spell was broken long before that. He could be talking to one woman, another would walk past, and there he would go.

Something about Antoinette had taken hold of him. Yes, he wanted to get her into bed, badly, but he was also just enjoying her company. He could listen to her talk for hours. Her voice was sweet but could take on a huskier quality when she was mad. There was a faint French accent just around the edges of a nearly perfect American accent that she'd no doubt honed over the years. She was smart and observant, and then there was the way she looked. Saying she was a classic beauty was an understatement. He almost worried that if he did bed her, he would lose interest, and then he'd have lost the most interesting person he'd ever met. This was saying a lot, as he'd been surrounded by interesting people since the day he was born.

Khaos could see her watching him from the corner of his eye, but he pretended to focus on the road ahead when all he could think of was her.

"Well, I'm waiting," she said, her breath sweet next to his ear.

He stifled a pleasurable shiver. She was waiting for him to talk more about his aunt and uncle.

"Fosette is a Frenchwoman, like you, born in the early 1700s. When were you born?"

"1721."

He glanced over at her. "The two of you will have much in common, I'm sure. No doubt she'll be fascinated to speak with you."

"She's immortal, but not a vampire?"

Khaos shook his head. "Not a vampire. She would have hated that. She's a witch, as I've said, a powerful one. As is her husband, Lucian. With my mother's help, they were able to create a spell of immortality long ago. They and their two sons have used the spell."

"How did your mother help?"

"My mother spends three months of the year in the Underworld with her mother, Persephone. While down there, many years ago, she came across Charon, the man who ferries the souls of the dead across the Rivers Styx and Acheron. They struck up an unlikely friendship. During one of their many talks, Charon told my mother that the stones from the bottom of these rivers could be used to prolong mortal life. Mom, who very much wanted to keep her mortal friends alive, wasted no time. She gathered those rocks and took them back to Fosette and Lucian. From those rocks, the spell was created."

"Fascinating. I imagine you have quite a few strange stories to tell."

Khaos laughed. "More than a few, I assure you."

"And they live in the swamp because that's where their power comes from?"

"More or less. Their power comes from nature, so, technically, they could live anywhere, but you don't get much more natural than the bayou."

"I guess not." Antoinette tapped a finger on her thigh. "What else do I need to know about them?"

"Not much, just that they're kind and good. Fosette is warm and lovely. Even though they live in the middle of nowhere, she always wears the prettiest clothes. Clothes she designs herself. And she bakes the most heavenly loaves of bread you've ever tasted. And Lucian, well, when he can peel his eyes from Fosette, he is just as kind and inviting. You'll love them both."

Khaos could feel Antoinette's eyes on him again. He wondered what she was thinking, wondered if she thought it strange that a man such as him could express such feelings for other people. His family seemed to forget that he did in fact possess actual feelings. He didn't do much to prove them otherwise, but he didn't want Antoinette to think him heartless.

Khaos pressed harder on the gas pedal. They had moved past the city limits and were now careening down smaller roads on their way into the bayou. It was darker without the glare from streetlights and bright signs. Khaos wasn't sure why, but he started to breathe a little easier. He loved the bustle of the city but loved the calm of these outer regions just as much.

"It's so peaceful out here." Antoinette echoed his thoughts. Her right hand rested on the interior door paneling, her delicate fingers loosely wrapped around the handle.

Khaos took his eyes off the road for only a second to look at her. When he gazed back, a woman stood in the middle of the road.

"Shit," he swore, slamming on the brakes.

Antoinette gasped as she held on to her seat for dear life.

The car slid to a stop, the wheels sliding a bit in the gravel, but the woman was gone.

"I didn't hit her. I know I didn't," he said, his head on a swivel looking from side to side, and his hand went to the door handle.

"Stop." Antoinette grabbed his arm. "Don't open the door."

She punched the door lock, but the doors were already locked.

"Why?"

She glared at him in the dark. They were now in the bayou proper, thick foliage from the trees and bushes on both sides of the road. "Haven't you ever seen a horror movie?" Her grip on his arm didn't let up. "The second you get out of the car to investigate, your Achilles tendon gets slashed or you get hit in the head with a baseball bat."

"Neither of those situations would keep me down for long. I'm a demon, remember? I can't be killed."

"So you think. We should continue on."

"Do you think it was her?"

"Jadis, the witch bitch who beat me up outside of the Comte's house? Yes, yes, I do."

"But you didn't see her?"

Antoinette shook her head. "No. By the time I looked at the road, there was nothing there. What did she look like?"

"Tall and willowy with hair longer and whiter than Gandalf after he returned from fighting the Balrog."

"Sounds like her, and it sounds like she wants to stop us from going any further. If we get out of this car, we're playing right into her hands."

Khaos broke eye contact with Antoinette. He looked all around them, then twisted himself around to peer through the back window. There was nothing and the night was as silent as a tomb. "I think you're right. Let's press on. We're almost there. Whoever she is, Jadis is not a match for both Fosette and Lucian. With the two of us in the mix, she'd be an idiot to try anything."

"Exactly, keep driving." Antoinette eased her grip but didn't let go.

Khaos was glad for the reassuring pressure of her hand.

He moved the car back in gear and stepped on the gas. The car sputtered forward a couple of inches, then lurched to a stop.

"What's happening?" Antoinette's grip tightened once more.

"I don't know." He tried again, but the car, which was still running, didn't move.

"Damn it." He turned off the engine, counted to ten, then pressed the button to restart the car. Nothing happened. "Well, now we're fucked."

"I told you." She removed her hand from his arm, crossing her arms in front of her chest. "You should have kept driving."

"And possibly run over an innocent human?"

She looked at him, fire in her gaze, her mouth a hard line. "What sort of innocent human stands in the middle of a road out in the bayou where no one could see her until it was too late?"

"Decent point, but a moot one. The car is dead, and we're stuck, exactly like the witch wanted."

"I still don't like the idea of getting out of the car. Can you call your aunt and uncle?"

"Great idea." Khaos pulled his phone from his pocket, but when he touched the screen to wake it up, nothing happened. "I really hate whoever this woman is."

"Why?" Antoinette glanced at his phone, then reached into her overnight bag to pull out her own. She tapped the screen. Then tapped it again and again.

"It's not going to work, Antoinette."

"What do we do?" There was a high-pitched panic in her voice.

Khaos wanted to touch her, wanted to place a reassuring hand on her thigh or her arm, but he didn't dare. He didn't know her well enough for that. And truth be told, he was a little panicked himself. "I know what we can't do, and that's stay here. No matter how much we may not want to leave the relative safety of the car, we have to."

"How far are we?" She slipped her phone back into her bag.

"We're about ten minutes by car. Two immortal beings, on foot, we could make in fifteen, maybe twenty. It's two against one, we'll make it. She may just be trying to scare us."

"Well, it's working because I'm scared. And you're assuming that she's alone. You know what they say about assuming. I, for one, don't think she could possibly be operating alone. And she was strong; she very nearly handed me my ass."

"True." Khaos took a deep breath before pocketing his phone and his keys. "Okay, grab your bag. We're going to run for it. Think you can keep up?" He grinned over at her, hoping that his shit-eating grin would annoy her enough to get her blood pumping.

She glared at him through half-lowered lids. "You're about to eat my dust."

He nodded, his hand on the door handle. "On the count of three. One, two, three." On three, they leaped from the car, slamming the doors behind them and taking off down the bayou road.

They didn't make it far.

After running for about thirty seconds, Jadis materialized in front of them, causing them to slide to a stop the same as the car had.

Khaos stood, his hands in fists down at his sides. He wanted to push Antoinette behind him but resisted. This wasn't the 1700s, and he doubted she would have appreciated the gesture. Instead, he tried another tactic.

"This is the witch causing all the mayhem?" He chuckled. "She's as skinny as you are." He glared, puffing himself up to his full demon height.

The witch cocked her white-haired head to the side as she took his measure. "Big things come in small packages."

Khaos laughed. "And bigger things come in bigger packages. We'll be going now." He reached out to take Antoinette's arm, but before he could move around the witch, pain stabbed him in the abdomen, and he doubled over with a grunt.

Antoinette moved to him, her arms going around him as she tried to pull him back up. "What are you doing to him? I told you I don't have the jewels. I'm looking for them the same as you."

"Yes, I know, and I told him that, but still, he's not convinced."

"I don't know who you mean. Who's not convinced?" Antoinette's arms didn't reach all the way around Khaos, but she tried to hug him to her all the same while she stared at Jadis.

The witch smiled, her teeth yellow, crooked, and wrong like her. "You really don't know, do you, little Madame?"

Khaos righted himself even though the pain in his stomach was agony. Something wasn't right. There was another player, and the way Antoinette had gone rigid next to him, told him she knew who this other person was.

"Tell me plainly. Who are you talking about?"

"The Comte St. Germain, of course."

AD BRAZEAU

CHAPTER ELEVEN

Antoinette felt the air go out of her lungs as if she'd been punched. She stood in the road, the bright lights from Khaos's car flooding around her, illuminating Jadis before her.

She narrowed her eyes, thoughts flooding her mind. The Comte couldn't possibly be alive. All those years ago, the police who'd come to take him away knew what he was. They knew he was unnatural, and they'd disposed of him. She'd been told as much by the young policeman, Officer Neville. After returning to New Orleans, she'd gone to the station to inquire as to what had happened. She'd mesmerized the officer into telling her everything. Officer Neville had told her that the Comte had been held in chains, decapitated, his body incinerated, and his ashes thrown in the Mississippi River.

Vampires may be immortal, but there was no coming back from that. She'd had no reason to not believe Officer Neville.

Antoinette shook her head, a sort of rough laugh escaping her lips. "Good one. You almost had me. Why don't you tell me something a little more useful?"

"Something more useful than the fact that your old lover has returned for you?"

Antoinette winced at the word *lover*. Ignoring the comment, she continued, "Yes. You could tell me who you are and why you want my jewels."

"As I've already told you, my name is Jadis, although that matters little, and again, I've already told you, I don't want the jewels, he does, and the why matters little to me. I'll have all I want after the Comte gets his due."

Khaos shifted next to Antoinette his boot heels grinding into the dirt. "I think I've heard enough. Have you?"

"More than enough," Antoinette answered.

Jadis laughed so loudly that an owl took flight from a nearby tree. "I don't care how you feel. What I care about are the jewels, and her." Jadis leveled Antoinette with a death glare. "My orders are to bring her with me, alive. You, on the other hand"—Jadis turned her gaze onto Khaos— "are expendable."

Antoinette glanced at Khaos, who stood stock still with an amused expression lighting up his eyes. "I've already mentioned that I don't think you'll be much of a match for me, witch. You're as thin as one of my fingers."

Jadis smiled in a way that chilled Antoinette to her bones. "And I already said that size matters little where I'm concerned."

With that, Jadis raised her hands. Antoinette knew that the witch was not only physically stronger than she looked but she was magical, something Antoinette wasn't. Khaos, on the other hand, was a demon, but he'd yet to display any magic.

Antoinette kept her attention on the witch and was glad she did. As soon as Jadis finished raising her hands in the air, her fingertips sparked with yellow flame.

Antoinette's questions were answered as to whether or not Khaos was magical when he turned, picking her up like she weighed nothing more than a football, and rushed into the dense swampland.

"Where are we going?" she asked as he jostled her about.

"Away from the witch with the fiery fingertips."

"Good idea." Antoinette held onto Khaos's bicep as he ran faster than even she could, dodging low-hanging branches and jumping over roots and goddess knew what else with the litheness of an Olympian.

Behind them, the night erupted into a bright white light. Jadis screamed, and then all was silent.

Khaos skidded to a stop. "Did you hear that?" he asked her.

"I think our witch screamed."

"I'll be damned." He turned, Antoinette still clutched in his arms, and squinted through the dark bayou.

"Khaos!" A female voice yelled in the night.

"Aunt Fosette! We're here." Khaos set Antoinette on her feet, though she wished he hadn't. The swamp slithered and splashed around them. Although they were on dry ground, and she couldn't be killed by a venomous snake or an alligator, she knew the night was alive, and this still made her nervous.

She reached out a hand for Khaos, fisting the back of his sweater as he led the way.

He reached a hand behind him. "Don't worry. We're not far from the road. Creatures of the night know their kind. They'll leave us alone."

"I know. I don't like it, but I know."

He chuckled, and she said nothing more.

As they wound their way back, Antoinette argued with herself about the Comte.

It was a lie.

He isn't alive.

The witch was messing with me to get me to show my hand.

After a few minutes, they emerged from the brush. Antoinette was still holding onto Khaos's sweater for dear life, her gaze on the ground, when he twisted around, extricating himself from her grasp, then spun and took a tall woman in a flowy green dress in his arms.

While Khaos took his time holding on to the woman, Antoinette scanned the scene on the road, which was unchanged, except Jadis was gone, and two other people were in her place. Khaos spun the woman, obviously Aunt Fosette, around and around as she laughed, her face buried in his neck. A man, tall and slender, in khaki pants and a white sweatshirt, stood not far away, his hands in his pockets and an amused expression on his face. The man looked at her and thanks to the light from the car's headlights, she noticed he looked younger than she'd been when she was turned.

He held out a hand as he strode toward her. "Lucian."

Antoinette shook his hand. "Antoinette. It's nice to meet you, Lucian."

"Put me down, you brute," Fosette said, still in Khaos's arms. "You forget your strength. Are you trying to snap me in half?" she asked with a laugh.

Khaos set her on her feet, then walked away to hug Lucian. "It's wonderful to see you both. You've no idea how perfect your timing was."

"Oh, I think we know." Fosette smiled warmly at Antoinette, holding out a hand. "And as you know by now, I'm Fosette."

Fosette towered over Antoinette as they shook hands. She was so lovely and feminine that Antoinette was struck by her beauty. She, too, appeared quite young.

"Did you kill her?" Antoinette asked. She looked around the area and didn't see any proof that Jadis had ever existed.

Fosette shook her head. "No, we scared her away. I imagine she'll be back, which is why we should get home. You'll be safe there. The house and surrounding grounds are warded to the heavens. Hades himself couldn't get in."

"I wouldn't be so sure about that," Khaos said. "But Jadis won't be able to."

"Was that her name?" Lucian asked.

Khaos nodded. "Do you know her? And how did you know we needed help?"

"No, we don't know her," Lucian answered. "But it's always helpful to know the names of one's enemies. We felt a surge of negative energy and came to check it out."

Fosette glanced toward the Lamborghini. "Do you think the four of us can squeeze into that thing?"

"I'm not sure it will matter. It died when the witch showed up."

Lucian snapped his fingers and the engine revved to life. "Show off," Khaos said with a smile. "Pile in."

Ten minutes later they were pulling down a long drive. Antoinette stared out the window at the wonderland around her. Yes, they were in the swamp, but the grounds had been both neatly manicured and also left wild in some places, creating a Narnia-like effect. Antoinette had never seen anything so lovely. There were angel oaks with branches sprawling out every which way, some so low they brushed the ground. There were trimmed, symmetrical hedges behind beds of colorful wildflowers, but the best part of all was the house. Khaos drove around the circular drive, a fountain with a faun sculpture at the center, parking in front of a home Antoinette was sure should be featured in *Architectural Digest*.

"This is not the swamp shack I was expecting," she said.

Lucian and Fosette laughed from the back seat where they were crammed in together.

Fosette said, "You should have seen the first home we shared out here. That shack didn't even have indoor plumbing. Of course, that was almost three hundred years ago."

Antoinette stepped out of the car, holding out a helping hand to Fosette. "You've been together for three hundred years? And you still like each other?"

Fosette laughed again. Antoinette liked her laugh, it was deep and genuine. "Well, we've had our moments, but for the most part, yes."

Antoinette marveled at a couple who could love each other for so long as she stared up at their beautiful house. The stone building was a miniature French chateau, which made her feel right at home. She'd almost forgotten that Fosette was French.

Fosette led the way through the front door. When everyone was inside the foyer, a giant crystal chandelier swaying over their heads, Lucian threw a massive iron deadbolt, sealing them all inside. Antoinette couldn't see the spells they had working to protect their home, but an iron deadbolt was a tangible thing that made her feel extra secure.

Fosette continued to lead them on as they strode past a formal sitting room and a library before entering a comfortable, less formal space. Khaos collapsed onto a giant, sage-green sectional. He kicked off his boots as if he were right at home and put his feet up on the cherry wood coffee table like he'd done this a thousand times.

He probably has.

Lucian sat in a rocking chair by a large picture window, snatching up a pipe as he did so. "Well, where do we begin?"

Fosette gestured for Antoinette to sit next to Khaos, then said, "We begin with refreshments. I'm going to get some coffee and cookies. Nobody says anything important until I return." She turned on her heel and left the room.

Lucian sucked on his unlit pipe, rocking in his chair. Antoinette wanted to laugh but didn't. Here was a man who appeared no older than twenty-five, with the habits of an old man. She was happy for the momentary silence, happy for a moment to gather her thoughts, but less than three minutes later, Fosette was striding back into the room with a tray laden with goodies. She set the tray on the table, shooing Khaos's feet onto the ground. There was a silver coffeepot, steaming from the spout, four floral china cups, a plate of chocolate chip cookies, and a stack of white cloth napkins.

Fosette handed out napkins, passed around the plate of

cookies, and then began to pour out the coffee.

Antoinette said no to the cookie but held out her hand for a steaming cup. The rich aroma of the grounds nearly made her head swoon. She inhaled deeply before taking a swig of the deep black goodness.

"Antoinette takes her coffee like the rest of us. Straight up. I like her already." Fosette sat in a Queen Anne armchair near the cold fireplace.

"You and Antoinette have a lot in common, Auntie," Khaos said with a smirk.

"Do we? Besides our coffee, what else do we have in common? Our love for a certain demon brat?" She blew over the top of her cup.

Antoinette nearly choked on her drink at Fosette's last statement. "Definitely not that."

She knew Khaos was about to spill the secret of her identity, and there wasn't much she could do about it, nor much she wanted to do about it. She'd spent so long concealing her identity, so long hiding in the shadows. Maybe she wanted a little of what Khaos had—comradery, and family.

Khaos, munching on a mouthful of cookie, swallowed before continuing. "You're looking at a bonafide historical celebrity, Auntie, straight from your home country."

Fosette sat straighter in her chair. "Not Marie Antoinette?"

Antoinette shook her head. "No, she was Austrian, although she molded herself into a perfect French queen. No, I'm another Antoinette, mistress to her father-in-law."

"Madame de Pompadour," Fosette breathed. "How incredible. I'm guessing this is going to be quite the story."

"Auntie," Khaos said as he picked up his coffee cup and resettled himself on the sofa. "You've no idea."

"Well"—Fosette smiled at Antoinette—"we're honored to have you in our home and happy to be able to help you, so anything you can tell us about your life and predicament will help us determine our next course of action."

And so, Antoinette began her tale.

CHAPTER TWELVE

Dawn was nearly upon them when Antoinette had finished telling Fosette and Lucian her story. No one, other than Antoinette, had spoken for hours, and Fosette and Lucian listened with bated breath from start to finish.

When she finally finished and sat back, Khaos thought over everything she'd said about her time with the Comte and the jewels. There was something different about the way she described the jewels this time, something that had stuck out to him.

Fosette opened her mouth, but Khaos leaned forward, cutting her off before she could begin. He had to get to the bottom of this. "Your story is as fascinating the second time around. There's just one thing that caught me a bit off-guard. When talking about the jewels, you mentioned an opal brooch, set in gold that was particularly dear to you." Khaos stopped long enough to regard Antoinette. If he wasn't mistaken, she'd squirmed. "You never mentioned this opal before. Why is this one piece of jewelry so dear?" He cocked his head to the side, watching her face intently.

She nibbled on her lower lip, a frown marring her features. She was uncomfortable with the question, but why? If the opal was merely of sentimental value, why not say so? Khaos leaned toward her. This was a tactic he'd learned as a young demon. When you had size on your side, you could use it to intimidate others into spilling their secrets. It seldom failed.

Antoinette couldn't hold his gaze. She stared down at her hands as she fumbled with a loose thread in her lap.

"What are you not telling us about the opal, Antoinette?" Khaos moved closer by another inch. She was hiding something, and before he went any further, he had to know what.

"Khaos, perhaps Antoinette has a personal reason for holding the opal dear." Fosette's voice was soft, low.

Khaos shook his head. "I don't think so. My instinct tells me there's another reason why the opal is important. What is it, Antoinette?"

"Fine." Antoinette looked into his eyes with a hard stare. "The opal is magical. That's why it's so important."

Khaos nodded. This was something he could understand. "Okay, what sort of magic does the jewel possess?"

"The cure to vampirism."

Khaos scoffed, leaning away from Antoinette. Fosette sucked in an audible gasp.

"You have to be joking," Khaos said, shaking his head. He almost laughed but checked himself.

"Do I look like I'm laughing?" Antoinette looked the opposite of amused, her mouth a flat line, her eyes narrowed.

"You had a jewel in your possession that contained a magical cure to vampirism?"

"I did."

Khaos leaned back against the armrest. His mind drowned in so many thoughts, that he had to take a moment and think about what to say next. He'd never heard of such a thing in all his long life. Surely, if there had been a cure for vampirism, Fosette and Lucian would have found one for

Desiree years ago.

"How did you get the cure, Antoinette? Who gave it to you?"

"I procured it from a French Quarter witch during my time with the Comte. I had originally meant to use it on him. Make him human and then kill him, but once the opal was no longer in my possession, I realized what I really wanted the cure for."

"Which was what?"

"Myself."

Khaos was dumbstruck. There were so many questions to ask, but more than anything, he was angry that she'd kept this important intel from him. He felt as if they'd become partners in the last couple of days, and this was not the kind of information you keep from a partner.

"Yourself?" He scoffed, again, pushing up from the sofa to stand with his arms crossed in front of his chest. "You didn't think this was key information? Is that why you've continued to look for it, because you want to be mortal?"

"It is. I've never felt suited to being a vampire. I would give anything to be human, to be able to live out a natural life and die. I've never been able to accept it. I've gone from one prison to the next, either someone else's or my own. I was only ever truly happy as a mortal."

"That sort of decision would certainly be a personal one, and one that you have every right to make for yourself," Fosette said, glancing from Khaos to Antoinette. "But tell me, dear, do you think the Comte knows about the opal, about what it can do?"

Antoinette shrugged. "I'm not sure. If he does, I've no idea how he found out."

Lucian rocked in his chair. "I think we should assume that he does know. He has a witch working for him, after all. Assuming he's aware of the power of the opal, he may want it for his own nefarious purposes. You said yourself that you originally wanted to use the jewel to kill him. It's not a leap to believe he also has murder on his mind."

"Antoinette's?" Khaos asked, meeting Lucian's eye.

"Anyone's. But whatever the reason for what the Comte wants with the jewels, it's clear that we can't allow him to find them. We've got to beat him to the punch. What leads do you have?"

"Only the policemen who came to the house that night. They're the only ones who could have had access to the jewels," Antoinette answered.

"What about the witch who created the spell?"

Antoinette shrugged, again. "It's possible. We could add her to the short list of suspects and check out her old home and descendants."

"She could still be alive," Fosette said. "We are."

Lucian continued rocking in his chair. "It's true. Since time seems to be of the essence, I suggest we divide and conquer. Fosette and I will investigate this French Quarter witch, while you two start with the policemen who were at the Comte's home the night he supposedly died."

Fosette stood. "Since daylight is almost upon us, Antoinette isn't going anywhere until dusk. I suggest she and Khaos get some sleep. We'll reconvene tomorrow night."

After getting the name and location of Antoinette's French Quarter witch, Fosette showed Khaos and Antoinette upstairs. Khaos moved toward his usual room, a back bedroom with a view of the garden and swamplands, while Fosette ushered Antoinette toward the room next to his.

"There are fresh sheets on all the beds and fresh towels in the en suite bathrooms. Please make yourself at home, I know Khaos will. Feel free to shower, take a hot bath, poke around the kitchen, whatever you like." Fosette patted Antoinette on her shoulder, then turned to hug Khaos. "Don't give her a hard time," she said in his ear. "We all have secrets." She released him, moving to head back down the stairs.

Antoinette leaned against the door frame, her gaze

wandering around the wide-open space of the second floor. "Again, when you said your aunt and uncle live in the swamp, this was not what I pictured."

"Yeah." Khaos watched Fosette as she disappeared down the stairs to avoid looking at Antoinette.

"I'm sorry I didn't tell you."

Khaos bit the inside of his cheek, his gaze moving from the empty staircase to Antoinette's feet. His mind was still racing with questions. He didn't trust people easily. Even though he'd been brought up in a loving household with people who would lay down their lives for him, he'd still been born in the Underworld, where he'd spent his formative years. The Underworld was a place for liars, manipulators, and users of all kinds. It was easier to keep people at arm's length.

"Well, you should have. I don't mind putting myself in harm's way, but I have a serious problem with Fosette and Lucian being dragged into this mess. A mess that we can't even fully define."

"I get it. All I can do is apologize. I don't trust easily."

Khaos looked at her then. He'd just been thinking the same thing. They were so similar in some ways, both untrusting, both cautious. Antoinette looked so small to him as they stood in the dark hallway. The only light came from a window at the far end of the hall. Light from the exterior gas lamp shone through the glass, filtering over the portraits of various family members hanging in the hall. There was his mother and father, his aunts and uncles. He had more than he realized, more than just money. He had people. Something Antoinette didn't.

She gazed up at him, her eyes tired.

"I understand," he said, his tone softening. "I haven't always been the most trusting, either. Although I should be. I've been lucky enough to be surrounded by trust and love for the majority of my life."

"You are lucky. I haven't had a family in so long. Eternity is endlessly lonely when you're all alone in the world."

Khaos didn't know what to say. The way Antoinette looked in the soft light, the shadows softening her features all the more, nearly melted his heart. What he wanted to do was pull her into his arms. He realized it had been days since he'd had a woman. Days may not have been long for the average bear, but Khaos was far from average. He also realized that he didn't want just any woman. No longer would anyone do to warm his arms and his bed. He wanted her, but did she want him? He doubted very much that she did. She wanted to be mortal, something he couldn't be, not ever. There wasn't enough magic on earth that could change him.

"Fosette was right. You should get some rest."

Her eyes were near to closing. Antoinette had never looked so beautiful to him in her calm near repose in the hallway. Her silky straight hair lay over her shoulder like a waterfall he longed to run his hands through. The faint pink of her cheeks deepened as she met his eyes once again.

Khaos stirred. Was she moved by him, or was the flush due to exhaustion? The man he was last week would have taken every advantage. He would have pulled her into his arms and made her his, even if just for the night. But he didn't want to do that. Not now, not with her. She was far more valuable to him than a one-night stand. Could a man change so much in so short a time? Perhaps a man could, but could a demon? Had he learned to value another person's feelings and well-being over his own?

He grumbled, shifting from one foot to the other. His thoughts were beginning to sound like some heroes in a romance novel. Khaos was no hero, nor did he want to be. He squeezed his eyes shut, reminding himself that what he truly wanted was to go back to normal. To have free reign with his fortune, to come and go from the family mansion as he pleased, to go back to his life of pleasure. He certainly didn't want anything resembling romantic love.

He took a step back. Shocked by his thoughts.

"What's wrong?" Antoinette asked. "You went somewhere else."

Reality seeped back in as Khaos opened his eyes. "I guess even demons get tired. Get some sleep and we'll start with your old-timey policeman list when the sun sets."

Something like disappointment seemed to flicker across Antoinette's face before responding. "Sure. We'll start with the one named Neville and go from there. Goodnight, Khaos." She lingered for a moment in the hall before stepping into the room.

"One sec, you two." Lucian rushed up the stairs. "We have a little something for you." He looked from Antoinette to Khaos. "Uh, sorry. Did I interrupt something?"

"No," Khaos barked.

Lucian's eyes went wide. "Okay." He handed a small piece of wood hanging from a leather string to Antoinette and one to Khaos. "These pieces of swamp oak have been enchanted with a spell. The spell won't last forever, maybe a couple of days, but it will shield you from anyone trying to locate you through magic. Wear them around your necks starting now. Don't take them off until I say so."

Antoinette did as Lucian said and slipped hers over her head. "Thank you, Lucian. This will provide some peace of mind tomorrow night while we're skulking around town."

"That's the idea. Our hope is this cloaking spell will shield you both and give us time to find the answers you seek. It might even give us the time to find the opal before the Comte." Lucian nodded. "Goodnight." Then he disappeared back down the stairs as quickly as he'd appeared.

Antoinette melted Khaos with one last look before she, too, disappeared into the dark. "Goodnight, Khaos."

AD BRAZEAU

CHAPTER THIRTEEN

Antoinette was up with the moon, as always. She was not a late sleeper, even when nothing of note was happening in her long and solitary life. Even when she'd had a hard time falling asleep as she'd had the morning before.

Khaos had been annoyed with her, maybe even angry for not telling him about the opal. A pit formed in her stomach at the thought that she may have pushed him away when she was just starting to like him.

Her cheeks flushed, her body warming at the thought.

I don't like him like that.

She tried to deny the sensations in her body as she brushed her hair. Khaos was a demon, end of story. She didn't want to get physically involved with a demon, she wanted to be mortal. A mortal woman and a demon were not compatible. He could undoubtedly warm her bed for a night or two, but a demon was not suitable for long-term companionship. Antoinette was a long-term kind of girl.

When she'd re-dressed in the same clothes she'd worn the night before, pulled her long hair into a sleek ponytail, and pinched her pale cheeks, she went downstairs in search of Khaos.

She found him pacing in the foyer in front of the open front door.

"Is everything okay?" she asked.

He stared down at his phone, not bothering to look at her. "I'm beginning to think this was a bad idea."

"What?" The pit in her stomach grew into a boulder.

"Fosette and Lucian are staying near Kenner tonight. They haven't located your witch, but they did catch wind of a descendant near there. They're going to look her up in the morning."

Antoinette was learning how to read Khaos and his many moods. He was agitated. Not only was he pacing, his gaze anywhere but on her, his shoulders were rigid as he moved, and he was chewing on his bottom lip.

She rested her hand on the staircase railing. "What's wrong with that? Kenner isn't far. They've been in contact and are safe. It doesn't seem like they're taking unnecessary risks."

When he finally looked at her, there was fire in his eyes, and she knew she'd said the wrong thing, her already queasy stomach dropping.

"They're safe? My aunt and uncle are the very opposite of safe, Antoinette. They're out searching for a witch that may be involved with someone who wants you dead. I should not have let them go. I'm an idiot for even being involved in any of this." He shoved his phone into his back pocket. "I want you to be okay, but I can't risk my family, too. I've let myself get swept up in all this, in you, but this is perhaps part of what my parents always cautioned me on. I'm thinking too fast, not slowing down to consider all the implications, and taking risks with my family."

She wasn't his family. The message was loud and clear. Antoinette bit back the tide of unexpected emotion that threatened to spill over. Why she felt upset at an obvious truth was confusing her. Did she want to be his family? Was she beginning to hope that maybe she had found the thing she'd been so lonely for? "I understand. I should never have put anyone else in danger." She moved past him, out the open front door, and into the fresh air. She closed her eyes, inhaling the deep, earthy scent of the bayou.

"I want to help you, Antoinette. I do. I just have a bad feeling." Khaos was behind her, his boots crunching the gravel of the drive. His voice had softened, but the damage was done. He started to speak again, but Antoinette cut him off.

She whirled around. It was best to push him away. He was right. It was unfair of her to ask his family, people who didn't know her from Eve, to help her fight a battle with no clear course. To fight any battle at all. He would continue to follow her around if she didn't make it clear that she didn't want his help. She was going to have to say things that she didn't mean. It was the only way and not the first time she'd had to do this.

"I did a lot of thinking last night, and I've decided that I don't want your help. Or theirs. They don't know me. Fosette and Lucian heard the story of my life summed up into a twenty-minute speech. They don't know the real me, nor would they probably care to. Text them and tell them that I've found the witch and will be pursuing this on my own. I don't want their help, and I don't want yours. I mean"—she scoffed, something she'd learned from Khaos over the last couple of days—"you're a demon. What good are you to anyone?"

The look on his face nearly sent her to her knees. His eyes widened, his brows pinching together. At first, she thought he was angry and was going to tell her off. It was worse when he didn't say anything at all. He simply looked at his phone, typed out a message, and hit *Send*. He didn't look at her again. He returned the phone to his back pocket, walked around the car, and opened the door.

Half inside and half out, he looked over the roof of the automobile at her. "I'll take you home, then please accept my resignation."

Antoinette hadn't cried in many, many years, but she

nearly cried then. The back of her throat burned like hellfire, tears pooling in her eyes. If she blinked, they would fall. She bit the inside of her lip as hard as she could and dug her nails into the palm of her hand, a trick she'd learned as a mortal to keep herself from crying in front of others.

She simply nodded, opened the door, and sank into the passenger seat of Khaos's car. The drive would be long and awkward, but it was better this way. She was better on her own. This was something she'd known all her life. Even as the king's mistress, surrounded by the court, her life was a solitary one. No one knew the real her. Not the king, not the ladies who smiled at her face, then sneered behind her back, no one. This was why she had to become mortal. Another two hundred years alone was unfathomable.

The drive back to New Orleans was exactly as Antoinette had predicted—tense. Khaos hadn't spoken a single word to her, nor she to him. She'd simply stared out the window, nails pressed into the palm of her hand to keep the emotions at bay. All the way home, she repeated one mantra over and over to herself.

I don't need anyone.

I don't need anyone.

The second Khaos pulled into the alley behind Noir, Antoinette's hand curled around the release. Before the car could come to a complete stop, the door was opened, and she was stepping out. She slammed the door behind her, then trotted through the tiny courtyard to the security pad. She punched in her code and escaped into the cool darkness of her home. Once the door was securely closed behind her, she slumped against it, sliding down to the floor. Only then did she allow the feelings welling inside her to finally spill over.

With her head leaning against the cool metal of the door, her hands by her side, she let herself cry with abandon. Tears streaked down her face, her eyes squeezed shut so tight they hurt, her head pounding with pressure. Antoinette couldn't remember the last time she'd cried. The last time tears ran down her face may very well have been over the death of the king. Antoinette wasn't one for emotion, but she knew that if she let the tears fall, she would feel better. Then, she could regroup and start again in her search for the jewels. For the one jewel, really. The jewel that would set her free from the never-ending nightmare of the blood.

But, as luck would have it, she'd have to pull herself together sooner than she'd anticipated when her vampiric ears picked up the sound of footsteps heading toward the office. She knew those footsteps and could easily recognize them out amongst the cacophony of the club. Deena was on her way to the back of the house, probably to see if she'd come in.

Antoinette jumped to her feet with the litheness of a cat, smeared the back of her arm with her tears, and painted a serene smile on her face. Just as Antoinette reached the doorway of her office, Deena was coming down the opposite end of the hall. As she walked inside her sanctuary, music from the club thumped in behind her, laughter and voices in conversation, just what Antoinette needed to bring her a much-needed sense of reality.

"Hey, boss," Deena said in her sing-song voice, a bright smile on her face. Deena, like Antoinette, wasn't much of a smiler. On a normal day, Antoinette would inquire as to what, or who had made Deena so happy, but she didn't have the energy. Vampire, though she was.

"Hi," Antoinette answered, entering her office. She took three large strides to her desk chair and then slid into the seat.

"How was Baton Rouge?" Deena asked, following her inside.

Antoinette still had to keep up appearances, and she still had to act as if the bar were important to her. With a serene smile in place, she glanced up at Deena.

"Oh gods," Deena began, the bright smile fading a bit.

"You slept with him, didn't you?" Deena shook her head, her gaze finding the ceiling. "Girl, you can mess with who you want, but I'm telling you, that dude is trouble with a capital *T*."

"I'm aware, and no, I didn't sleep with him." Antoinette reached for her laptop; she had some investigating to do if she was going to find the family of Officer Neville and the witch who'd imbued the opal with magic.

"Speaking of Trouble, is he going to be working the door tonight? I have Elise on it right now, but we could use a big dude."

Shit, the door.

Antoinette opened the laptop, heaving a sigh as she did so. "I don't think Khaos is going to be back here. We're going to have to find someone else. I give you full leeway to hire who you need to, starting tonight. Pay them well, and maybe we can get someone right away."

Deena made a face, her lips pulling into a slight grimace. "Well, I can stroll down Bourbon and see if there's anyone I can poach from a different club."

"Normally, I would say no, but desperate times." Antoinette typed in her password. "Just make sure you keep it on the down-low. The last thing we need is the whole Quarter pissed at us. You know how people talk around here."

"No worries, boss. Leave it to me." Deena turned, leaving the office door open.

If Antoinette knew anything, it was that she could very well leave it to Deena and she would handle everything. Antoinette had been able to rely on Deena since day one.

After Antoinette's laptop fired to life, the screen illuminating her face in the darkened room, she found the browser and typed *Officer Neville, New Orleans PD, 1902.*

Antoinette was amazed by what she found. The modern age was truly miraculous. The first search result was an article from the *Times-Picayune*, dated November 4th, 1902, the day after the Comte's house had been raided. She skimmed through the article and came up with gold, literally.

The second to last paragraph of the article read: *Taken from the home were several items of great value including an oil painting by the Dutch master Rembrandt, Persian rugs, solid gold sconces from Paris, and a casket of jewels. These items are believed stolen and will be stored at the New Orleans Police Department until their original owners can be identified.*

Yes, the jewels were stolen, from me, Antoinette thought.

The article then spoke about the bravery of Officer Neville and his men, and that Officer Neville would likely receive a commendation for his service.

The next search result was an article about Officer Neville's commendation and promotion to Captain.

Result number three was an article titled *Theft at New Orleans Police Station.* Antoinette's stomach dropped. She knew what she was about to read. Sure enough, the jewels along with the Rembrandt had been stolen from the station. Antoinette was back to square one.

CHAPTER FOURTEEN

Khaos felt as if Antoinette had slammed a piece of his heart in the car door.

He wanted so badly to help her. Hell, he was beginning to feel as if he'd do anything for her, but sacrificing the safety of his family was not something he was willing to do. His family was the one thing he couldn't give.

His car idled in the alley as he stared after Antoinette. There was an ache in his body now that she was gone, a sensation pulling him toward her. He wanted to get out of the car, go inside Noir, and beg her forgiveness, but he didn't. He couldn't. He only trusted her about halfway. She'd lied about the opal, after all. What else had she lied about?

He glanced down at his phone. No reply from Lucian. He should have texted Fosette, as Lucian was known to be a little technologically inept.

Auntie, the mission has been aborted. Antoinette and I have parted ways. Please respond and let me know when you two are on the way back home.

Khaos tossed his phone on the passenger seat. He had little money and nowhere to go. His hands skimmed over the buttery leather of the steering wheel. The car was only his asset. As much as he hated to part with her, it was time to make big-boy decisions. There was a luxury used car lot in Metairie. He wouldn't get what the car was worth, he was prepared for that, but he'd at least get enough to stay in a nice hotel room for the day, then a decent apartment after that. The money would buy him time to find some sort of job. Hell, if he received half of what the car was worth, he might be able to buy a small apartment. He'd have to work, though. There was no way around that.

Khaos rolled his eyes at the thought of a job. Imagining a demon working for a living was ridiculous. Still, what choice did he have? His only other option was to return to the Underworld, something he'd never do.

He peeled out of the alley, his focus on anything and anyone besides Antoinette.

The car lot smelled like motor oil and pavement. The night was dark, the sky clear overhead.

Khaos had pulled into the lot about twenty minutes before close. There were two salespeople inside, a balding man slipping past middle age and a young woman in her late twenties. Khaos made a beeline for the woman.

She was pretty, just his type, with a lithe figure, large breasts, and fingernails so long and sharp that all he could think of was how they'd feel clawing his back. She stood as he walked toward her, opened her mouth to speak, then closed it as she took him in. He was used to this, the effect he had on women. Her gaze raked his body from stem to stern as she took in every inch of him. Her half-parted mouth twitched up at the corners as she met his eye.

"I was about to say that we're closing soon."

"But you decided against it?" He leaned against the side of her desk, making sure his massive pectorals were right in her line of sight.

She huffed out a breath. "How can I help you?"

He smiled, slyly. If he played his cards right, he not only might get top dollar for his car, but he might also get a much-needed release for all the tension coiled in the small of his back. He leaned closer as if he were about to impart a secret. "I need to sell my car."

"I can help you with that. Shall we take a look?" She glanced down at his crotch as she said the word *look*.

He smiled wider. "One thing at a time."

Thirty minutes later, Khaos had a check in his pocket and a breast in his right hand. The male salesperson hadn't needed much convincing to leave Sandy alone with a stranger, so they were now blissfully alone in the workroom. He'd gotten what he wanted and more for his precious car, taking the sting out of having to part with her. And now, he was about to get a whole lot more.

Sandy's behind was on the kitchenette counter, her elbow whacking the coffee maker as Khaos took a handful of her hair, pulling back her head so he could suck on her neck. For some reason, he couldn't get himself to kiss her on the lips, no matter how desperately she'd tried to kiss him.

He suckled what should have been tender, young flesh, but which instead felt hard and tasted far too salty. Antoinette and her perfect swan's neck flashed in his mind. He squeezed his eyes shut as if that would help and changed tactics. Instead of getting her worked up, he'd just go right for the prize. What more could you expect from a hookup like this?

He grabbed her hips, pulling her toward his, then reached down to unzip his fly. That's when the mistake was made. He looked into her eyes. Sandy's eyes were not Antoinette's eyes.

Sandy seemed annoyed that he hadn't made any progress, so she moaned as if she were enjoying herself and reached down to help him out. When her hand grazed the front of his pants, he stepped back.

"What's wrong?" she asked breathlessly. Why she was breathless was a mystery since they hadn't kissed, and they'd barely touched.

Khaos shook his head, about to apologize to the poor girl.

Instead, a female voice from behind him said, "Can't get it up?"

Khaos dropped his face into his hands with a groan. "Des, why are you here?"

"What is happening?" Sandy asked, her voice shaky. Her gaze moved over Desiree's fire-red hair, down her athletic figure clad in black leather.

"Nothing, dear." Desiree shoved Khaos to the side, moving to Sandy. She smoothed down the girl's hair. "You're going to get your things, lock up as usual, and go home. You bought this man's car, and he left. Do you understand?"

Sandy nodded like a child, sliding off the kitchen counter. Her bare feet hit the floor with a thud. Then she was gone.

"Well, this is embarrassing." Khaos sat on one of the remarkably small plastic chairs that sat around the sad workroom table.

"For you? I wholeheartedly agree." Desiree moved around the brightly lit room like a sprite opening cupboards and smelling tea packets. "What strange places offices are."

"When you're finished investigating how the muggles live, maybe you can focus and tell me what the fuck you're doing here." Khaos watched her open a drawer and finger the unseen contents. She was completely unbothered by him, as she was by most people.

"I wanted to see how you are. Fosette called me and said she and Lucian were out searching for the descendants of a witch who might be able to help you and Madame de Pompadour"—she looked at Khaos then, her eyebrows raised—"find some magical jewels?" The entire statement was a question.

"Yes, but I told them to cut it short and go home. The Madame and I are no longer acquainted."

"Figures." Desiree sank into the seat opposite him. "I mean, you're usually not acquainted with anyone for long. Although, it's a shame. I think I would have liked to meet Madame de Pompadour."

"Yes, well, as you've already pointed out …" Khaos moved his hand in the air, not bothering to finish his sentence.

"Which brings me to my second reason for seeking you out." Desiree stopped looking around the room to level him with an emerald-green stare. "When are you going to go home?"

Khaos laughed, loud and long. "Go home?" He feigned wiping a tear from his eye. "Perhaps you've forgotten that I've been unceremoniously thrown out of my home."

"You're acting like a spoiled child, not a two-thousand-year-old demon. You needed to learn a thing or two, and you and I both know that if you learn those things and go home, your parents will welcome you back with open arms."

Khaos looked down at his lap. There wasn't much he could say about that. Desiree wasn't wrong. He had been a spoiled child, had always been a spoiled child. Of course, his parents had tired of his antics. Hell, he was even tiring of his antics, as proven by the evening's failed dalliance.

He heaved a sigh, meeting the frank stare of his aunt. "I'll go back, but not yet."

She smiled at him, her gorgeous face lighting up like the sun. "Good. Your mother misses you, and so does Theron, even if he won't admit it out loud. He's been grumpier than normal lately."

Khaos chuckled at the thought of Theron missing anyone other than his mother, Greer. "You can report back that all is well. I have sold my stupid car and am going to do my best to care for myself, for now."

"That car was pretty stupid. An extension of your penis,

I believe a modern psychologist would say."

Khaos chuckled harder than he had in weeks, Desiree joining him with her throaty laugh.

"Okay, my little nephew." Desiree took his hand, hauling him to his feet alongside her. He was anything but little, towering over her as they stood. "Let's get out of this strange place. I'll even drop you off, wherever you'd like to go."

They slipped out an unlocked side door, Khaos grateful that Sandy had missed it. He didn't relish the thought of breaking a window to get out.

Desiree unlocked her old, 1980s Volvo, Khaos cramming himself into the small passenger seat.

"Now, on the way back to the city, you can tell me all about this Madame." Desiree started the car, her eyes on the road, a smile to beat hell on her face.

Khaos didn't think he'd be able to sleep, and he didn't. Desiree had dropped him at a decent mid-level hotel on the outskirts of the French Quarter. From the second Khaos stepped out of her car, he felt a pull to keep walking north to Chartres Street and right into the dark bar of Noir. It took all of his willpower to put one foot in front of the other in the direction of the hotel lobby.

He'd crawled into bed fully clothed, then spent the next two hours tossing and turning as he thought about Antoinette and what she was doing. Was she out searching for the opal, even now? Was she putting herself in more danger, or would she give up the chase with no one to help her? A pit formed in his stomach at the thought of her being alone. She had no one to aid her now. Only days ago, Khaos felt lonely for the first time in his life. It was not a good feeling. That feeling had been the worst, the lowest he'd ever felt in his life. Even though he'd felt alone, the fact was that after he'd been kicked out of his house, he still had people on his side. Aunt Desiree had sought him out to ensure he was okay, and Aunt Fosette and Uncle Lucian had taken in both him and Antoinette when they needed help.

Where are those two?

With all that had happened, he'd forgotten to check his phone. Plus, hadn't Desiree said she'd spoken to Fosette? Was that before or after Khaos had texted her?

He opened his text stream with Lucian. The text had delivered but had yet to be read. The same was true for Fosette. There were no new texts.

Having no other options, Khaos did something he never did. He swiped to Fosette's contact and called her.

The phone rang and rang. Voicemail.

He did the same with Lucian. No one answered.

Khaos sat up in the bed. He'd been too distracted to realize he hadn't heard from them since they left their house the day before. Where the hell were they?

Still restless and now worried, he began pacing the room. The low-level décor around him felt bleak. Although a big step up from the hell hole he'd flopped in on the fringes of the French Quarter, this place somehow seemed sadder. Everything was beige. Worn beige carpet, beige walls, knicks, and chips, revealing white drywall underneath, a beige coverlet on the bed, and a beige chair in the corner, a gross-looking brown stain on the seat. He could have splurged for something nicer but needed to hoard his money. Who knew when he'd get more? He had to chuckle at the thought of a demon in a family-friendly hotel.

Just as he was thinking about how much his mother would hate the décor, the phone came alive in his hand, the display glowing with a name he hadn't seen in a while.

He swiped to answer. "Keir, have you spoken to your parents?" Even if Khaos had been the type to engage in pleasantries, there wasn't time. Something felt wrong, urgent.

"That's why I'm calling you." Keir's deep voice was strained. Keir, the natural son of Fosette and Lucian, had been preserved in time as they had. By magic. He was forever twenty-one, as long as the magic remained intact. He and Khaos had been close as kids, raised closely together like cousins. They'd spent many of their early years side by side, but that had changed as they'd grown. Keir seemed less and less inclined to hang with Khaos the older, and wilder, he became. Keir was a nice guy, but he was strait-laced and square, a personality type Khaos found boring. Keir continued, "The last I heard from them was the other night. Dad texted to say that he and Mom were headed toward Kenner to locate the relations of an old New Orleans witch. He said he'd let me know when they were back. I was asleep, so I didn't get the text."

Of course you were.

Keir wasn't finished. "I didn't think much of it. I mean, they're witches, so why would I be concerned if they were seeking out others? But when I realized this morning that I hadn't heard from them, I kind of freaked out."

"I take it they're not answering your calls?" Khaos leaned against the headboard, fingers digging in the corners of his eyes. Why was he forever making wrong decisions in life?

"No. Do you know what's going on? Dad also mentioned in his text that they were helping you." There was an undercurrent of anger and annoyance in Keir's tone. An undercurrent Khaos was familiar with. People were often angry and annoyed with him.

"All I can do is bring you up to speed. After that, it's time I head toward Kenner myself to see what I can find."

Khaos told Keir the story from start to finish. He began with being kicked out of his house and ended with his and Antoinette's fight, and how he was now living in a hotel room until he could find a small apartment.

When he was finished, Keir sighed, the anger and annoyance still there. "I'm coming to get you. Then, you and I are picking up your vampire friend, and we're going to go find my parents."

Khaos began to protest, then realized no one was there.

Keir had hung up.

Fuck.

Khaos tossed his phone on the bed. He wondered if he should call Des or his mother. They should know that Fosette was in danger. Theron was the most powerful being in New Orleans. If someone needed help, it stood to reason that Theron should be the one to provide that help. But something held Khaos back. He'd been such a screw-up his entire life. If they found out that Fosette and Lucian were missing, likely in danger, and the reason for this was entirely Khaos's fault, well, they would have enough fuel for their disappointment to last them centuries.

No. Khaos would fix this himself.

He stripped off his days-old clothes, leaving them in a pile on the floor, and walked straight into the shower, letting the water get as hot as possible. He needed to sanitize every pore. He soaped and shampooed until his skin squeaked, then stepped out to rub himself hard with the stiff hotel towel. The bathroom was nicer than the bedroom. The tile on the floor was white and looked new, the bathtub-and-shower combo glowed as if freshly scrubbed.

Thank the gods Des had had the foresight of mind to ask if he needed to get anything out of his car before they left the dealership. What few things he had were now contained inside the duffle bag he tossed on the unmade bed. He pulled out a long-sleeved black Henley, a pair of clean boxer briefs, and a pair of black jeans. He dressed quickly, then pulled on black socks and his black combat boots, feeling as if he were dressing for war. He left his Cartier watch in the room's safe. One last thing to sell, if he needed to.

Just as he was pushing some product through his blow-dried black hair, there was a knock.

Khaos opened the door to reveal Keir. He was still fresh-faced, a kid of twenty-one, who, to Khaos, looked more like he was seventeen. He favored Fosette, which was lucky for him, his skin dark and his cheekbones sharp. He was tall and straight-backed, as was she, but he had Lucian's hazel-green eyes. Nowhere near as tall or as muscular as Khaos, Keir was still formidable to average-sized people.

Also formidable was the look of disdain in his eyes. A look straight from his uncle Theron.

"Let's go." Keir made a gesture with his hand and turned back around.

"Hold up, kid." Khaos could call him a kid because, to Khaos, everyone was a kid. He may have looked like a child when they grew up together, but in reality, he was anything but.

Keir turned back to face him. The look of disdain had taken on an angrier cast. "I'm not a kid. You may be a demon who's thousands of years old, but out of the two of us, I'm the more mature, by far." Keir crossed his arms. "You've done nothing but act like a deviant for centuries, while everyone else has had to go around and clean up your messes."

Khaos's blood warmed up, his cheeks getting hot. "No one else has had to clean up my messes." He knew this was a lie, but hoped Keir wasn't well-versed in the stories of his life.

"Really?" Keir's moved his hands to his hips. "How about the time you almost impregnated an entire bus full of Tulane cheerleaders?"

"I can't help that they couldn't keep their hands off me."

"Auntie Des had to hypnotize them all while my mother gave them a tea that would keep your seed from taking hold."

"I didn't ask for their help. Des was stalking me as usual." Khaos was beginning to feel defensive.

"Auntie Des *has* to stalk you, so you don't cause too much damage."

Khaos was a little stung by this omission. He thought Des was always around because she loved him like a son and only wanted to ensure he was safe and well. It seemed as if the joke had been on him. Des was always every which way he turned because he couldn't be trusted, and she felt the need to clean up after him. How exhausting that must have been for her over the centuries.

Khaos looked down at his hands, before shoving them in his pockets. "Well, she needn't worry any longer. And anyway, we have more pressing concerns."

"Yes, the disappearance of my parents."

"Have you told Des and the others?" By *others,* Khaos meant his parents.

"No. Your parents have enough on their hands. Not only that, but Auntie Des and Uncle Theron will go nuclear, and we need to recon first. We'll unleash them if we deem the situation necessary."

Khaos was stung, again, but didn't say anything. Keir was right. This whole thing was his fault. They never would have been in danger had he not sought them out in the first place.

Khaos inclined his head. "Let's go get Antoinette."

AD BRAZEAU

CHAPTER FIFTEEN

Antoinette sat up in her bed. She loved her little room in her little apartment, but the endless loneliness was getting to her. The endless night was getting to her. All she had to do was find that opal, and she could change the course of her life. She could wake up with the sun and feel its warmth on her skin. She could age naturally, live out the rest of her days, and be laid to rest. Rest was something she longed for. Rest would be a cure for the loneliness she felt.

Antoinette had a plan for the evening. She was going to seek out the French Quarter witch she'd engaged in 1902. Back then, the witch had lived in a Creole cottage on Burgundy, but Fosette and Lucian had been going to see a descendant in Kenner. So, that was where Antoinette would begin.

Antoinette wore a sleeveless navy blue top and cream pants and pinned her hair into a high bun. She longed to wear a dress, as the outdoor temperature was quite warm, but feared she'd be confronted by the Comte's witch again. If not the Comte himself, and if that were the case, she would need to be able to fight.

She slipped on tan loafers and headed down the stairs,

toward the business side of the building she owned. Noir was already jumping, music making the walls vibrate. Her employees, Deena especially, would begin to wonder what was going on. Deena was already suspicious of her, of that Antoinette was keenly aware, but she hoped that she could resolve the situation soon. Once she had the opal, she would make herself human, sign the business over to Deena, and go and live a very different sort of life. One much less nocturnal.

Without bothering to tell Deena where she was going, Antoinette walked out the back door and right into a massive chest.

She jumped back, knocking the side of her head on the metal doorframe. "Ow," she said, massaging her right temple.

Khaos stood in front of her, his hulking frame blocking out the artificial light behind him.

"What are you doing here?" She realized her question was rude, but, really, why was he there? To cause her more torment, no doubt.

"Nice to see you, too," Khaos said. There was a bubble of laughter behind him, but Antoinette couldn't see who it was. "We've come because we need your help."

"You need my help?"

A hand grabbed the side of Khaos's arm and pushed him aside. "Yes, strange, isn't it? Khaos doesn't usually ask for help, although plenty of people walk behind him with a mop. Metaphorically speaking, anyway."

"And you are?" Antoinette wondered if she had a concussion. Not only was Khaos here, asking her for help, but another man had seemingly materialized from behind him.

"Keir." The man held out a hand to her, which she took. "We're cousins, Khaos and I."

"Cousins," Antoinette repeated. Demons have cousins?

"Yes, Fosette and Lucian are my parents."

Realization dawned over Antoinette. "Oh, how are they?

They showed me such hospitality the other night. Such kind people."

If Antoinette wasn't mistaken, pain flashed in Keir's eyes. "They're missing. They went out to search for a witch, for you, I believe, and they haven't returned. Not only that, but they aren't answering texts or calls."

Antoinette's stomach dropped as nausea rolled through her belly. "They haven't returned?"

"No," Khaos answered. "We know they were headed toward Kenner, so that's where we're going. We could use your help locating them. This has Jadis written all over it."

"I'll do whatever I can." An ache bloomed in Antoinette's chest. How had she endangered so many people in such a short time? People who were not worthy of what she'd called down upon them. Whatever that was. She would have to put her investigation on the back burner and hope she wouldn't lose much time. The safety of Fosette and Lucian was paramount. Although, maybe finding the couple would lead her straight to the jewels.

She looked at Khaos, but he didn't seem to be looking at her so much as past her. She thought about last night and how painful the encounter with him had been. And then how the loneliness, always present in her life, had been nearly unbearable without his irksome presence. Khaos had affected her in the short time she'd known him, perhaps more than she'd like to admit.

"Where do we begin? Kenner?" Antoinette asked.

"My parents and I share our locations," Keir said. Khaos shot him a look, but Keir ignored him, and continued, "The last time I had a location for them, they weren't far. They were maybe twenty minutes outside the city, almost to the town of Kenner."

"Then let's go. We can't afford to lose another second." Antoinette made for the black SUV parked in her lot. She didn't see Khaos's ridiculous car with the non-existent back seat. She said a silent prayer of thanks for that. She was a small woman and yet she couldn't imagine cramming herself into the back of that sardine can. Neither of the tall men would have fit, that was for sure.

Although ahead of the men, Khaos somehow beat her to the car and held open the passenger door for her.

"I'll sit in the back," she said, avoiding his gaze. "Your legs are a lot longer than mine."

He caught her hand, holding it in his. She looked him in the eye. There was something there she couldn't quite define. Regret, maybe. All she knew was that his brow was pinched, his mouth a straight line. "I'd like you to sit in the front. You might see something that I'll miss."

Before she could respond, Keir called loudly from the driver's side of the car. "Yes, please sit in the front. I've known Khaos a long time and can easily say that I already trust your judgment over his."

Antoinette's hand lingered in Khaos's. He was warm, his palms soft despite his size. She didn't want to let go. There was something in this simple gesture of hand-holding that made her feel as if he could heal her wounds. But he set her fingertips on the inside of the door panel and moved behind her, toward the rear door.

Antoinette did her best to shake off the feelings at war within her. She'd missed him terribly, having become calmed by his presence the second she'd seen his face. Antoinette was reserved by nature, but being around Khaos made her want to jump into his arms and press her mouth against his. She couldn't do any of these things in front of Keir, so instead, she slid into the soft leather seat of the Land Rover, and said, "You probably shouldn't trust the person who's endangered your parents. If it wasn't for me, they would be safe at home."

"My parents make their own choices and, historically, make good ones. They wouldn't have bothered themselves with you if they hadn't found you worthy of their help." Keir started the car. "Now, let's get focused. I just want them back."

Thirty-four minutes later, the three of them were nearing the spot where Lucian's smartphone had last pinged. The traffic on this stretch of highway was light, making it easier for them to slow down and pay attention to any turn-offs they may need to investigate.

Antoinette had done her best to forget Khaos was behind her. At one point, he'd stretched out his leg, his knee grazing her elbow as it rested on the center console. Suddenly, her whole arm heated up, phantom flames licking her up to her collarbone. She'd had to tuck her elbow against her body and rub it repeatedly to dull the fire. What was it about this demon that gave her all the wrong ideas? Yes, he was gorgeous; anyone with eyes could see that, but there was more than that, and she knew it. When he was around, irritating though his presence could be, her loneliness was dimmed, maybe even forgotten, then the moment he left her, the dull ache in her chest would bloom all over again.

Antoinette was pulled from her thoughts by the sudden appearance of a turn-off. "There," she said a little loudly.

Keir jumped in his seat, she'd startled him, but he pressed on the brakes, slowing down so they could make the turn.

Khaos leaned forward, his breath hot in Antoinette's ear as he tried to see around her. She did all she could to block the feral heat that again sprang to life over her skin.

The turn-off was obscure, hidden well by a tangle of weeds and underbrush. Branches of live oaks shaded it overhead. Antoinette would have never seen it if it hadn't been for her vampiric eyes.

Keir made the turn, tires crunching gravel as the car went offroad, brush and tree limbs scraping the sides of Keir's nice SUV as they progressed.

"It certainly doesn't look like anyone has passed this way in some time," Khaos said, his breath moving Antoinette's hair.

"Any witch with even a modicum of skill could obliterate the signs of a car passing this way," Keir said. "Besides, look there." He pointed to a tree trunk they were about to pass. "It appears as if the mirror of a car scraped that tree."

Indeed, Antoinette could see a scar along the gray bark consistent with the height of a sedan-sized car. "We're on the right path," she said, touching the swamp oak amulet she still wore around her neck.

Where are they?

Minutes later, they pulled into a clearing. Though the canopy of oak trees was dense overhead, the brush had been cleared out to accommodate a small shack.

Keir stopped his car. They were around a hundred feet from the door of what appeared to be a one-room, log cabin. The windows were dark, no light shined inside, nor was there a light over the door. The only signs of life were the curls of smoke emanating from the chimney and the dark blue Volvo parked off to the side.

"That's my parents' car," Keir said as he turned off the engine.

Antoinette heard Khaos behind her. He'd shifted in his seat, reached for the door handle, and partially opened the door in less than two seconds.

"Hold on." Keir reached behind her. He must have grabbed hold of Khaos's arm because Antoinette heard Khaos pull away, Keir's fingers squeaking over the leather of Khaos's jacket. "We can't just go off half-cocked. We need to approach with caution."

"Keir ..." Antoinette could hear the sneer in Khaos's voice. "You do what you do best, which is to think, and I'll do what I do best, which is to act."

Antoinette, her eyes on the dark cabin, said, "Keir is right. We need to lead with our heads and not with our hearts."

Khaos gave in, and pulled the door closed with a soft click.

The night was so dark that the cabin, the smoke, and

even the trees around them appeared diaphanous. The tree canopy had cut them off from any light from the stars above. Nothing seemed real. Antoinette felt as if she was in the middle of a demented fairy tale. In her fairy tale, three paranormal beings are led into the woods, where an evil witch awaits. Will she roast them in her oven or chop them up and throw their pieces into a stew?

Antoinette continued, "We should fan out as we approach the cabin. One of us in the lead, the other two out to the sides, our attention on what could come from the shadows. We walk slowly, quietly, listening for any sound, looking for any danger, watching each other's backs."

"Do this kind of thing a lot, do you?" Keir asked.

"No, but I'm a quick study, and I recently learned that danger lurks where you least expect it and comes in packages that don't appear dangerous."

They exited the car as one, each of them slipping out as silently as possible, pressing their doors closed, rather than slamming them shut. Khaos took the lead. As the largest, most formidable being of the three of them, this was only natural. Antoinette peeled off to the right, Keir to the left. They held back, flanking Khaos while also giving him a head start of about ten feet.

Antoinette realized the car would have already been heard as it crunched down the overgrown path, but that was no reason to now go barreling up to the cabin door. The wrongness of the place hit her as soon as she laid eyes on it through the windshield. Now that she was outside, it hit her other senses, as well. There was an odd odor in the air. She couldn't tell what she was smelling, but whatever the scent, it was foul and bracken. Almost like a rotting fish caught in low tide. Not the earthy smells of tree bark and dirt one would expect from a wooded area. Not only was the smell off-putting but there was also no sound. The forest was silent. Antoinette had been around long enough to know that forests were alive with sound, even at night. They should have been able to hear owls hooting and bats squealing. Her preternatural ears should have picked up the skittering of bugs on tree limbs and the far-off sounds of cars on the highway, but there was nothing. It was almost like they were in a vacuum.

Antoinette shivered, goosebumps rising on her arms followed by a quiver in her belly. Her eyes couldn't adjust to the deep, dark night, no matter how hard she squinted. She hated not being able to see well, which was also strange. She should have been able to see clearly, even in the dark.

A sound off to her right alerted her to danger. She stopped walking and turned her whole attention toward what sounded like a step being taken in gravel. Her heart beat thunderously in her chest, which was ridiculous for a vampire but was true regardless.

She widened her stance, her gaze scanning the hazy darkness around her. The sound hadn't been far off. It had seemed as if someone had taken a step alongside her. But there was nothing, not that she could see, anyway. A chill raised the fine hairs on her arms. Frustration mounted. Her breath quickened, her brow aching with consternation.

She continued walking. Khaos was too far from her, so she picked up the pace, then looked over to the left. Keir was nowhere in sight. Where had he gone?

Dread settled at the base of her spine as she realized that she could no longer hear his footsteps. All she could hear was Khaos walking ahead of her along with the sound of her own steps in the gravel. They were still fifty feet from the cabin, and the plan had already gone to shit.

Antoinette wanted to scream out to him, but instead, she came to a stop, trying desperately to control her terror. "Khaos," she whisper-yelled at his back.

Khaos heard as well as she did, of this Antoinette was sure. She was proven right when he stopped and half-turned to see what she wanted. She pointed to the left and raised her shoulders, her mouth open with the silent question *Where is Keir?*

Khaos turned his back on the cabin. He looked off to

where Keir had been flanking him, then looked past Antoinette.

Shit, he mouthed. Khaos looked at Antoinette, fear in wide-open eyes. He held out a hand, beckoning her toward him.

She moved quickly. He didn't need to tell her twice that they were in danger, that they needed to find Keir. Their hands clasped tight the second they touched, and together they moved off toward where Keir should have been. It was Antoinette's sincere hope that they would find him examining something off to the side. His parents' car wasn't far off, after all. Maybe he'd gone to the car to see if he could find a clue. As one, Khaos and Antoinette moved in the direction of the Volvo.

Just as Antoinette suspected, the passenger door of the Volvo had been opened. She peered inside, Khaos still clutching her hand. The interior of the car appeared normal. Nothing was spilled or torn. There was no appearance of a fight having taken place or the occupants fleeing for their lives. The only thing inside, the one item that sent a chill down Antoinette's spine, was a smartphone that sat in a cupholder. There was no doubt it was Lucian's phone. The one that had pinged at this location.

Suddenly, there was a grunt behind them, causing Khaos to take Antoinette around the waist, and the two spun around together.

Antoinette's breath caught in the back of her throat, her heart all but stopping in her chest. There, not ten feet in front of the open cabin door, stood the witch Jadis, Keir kneeling before her. She held a knife to his throat with one hand as the other rested on his shoulder.

Khaos squeezed her hand before dropping it. Antoinette longed to be physically connected to him again but knew if they had to fight, hand-holding would not be practical.

Antoinette squared up her shoulders and hips, her hands clenched into fists at her sides.

I'll be damned if someone else gets hurt because of me.

She would not let Jadis hurt Keir, not for anything in the world. This family—Khaos, Keir, Fosette, and Lucian—they'd helped her when she'd had no one. They hadn't asked for anything in return, and she would do her best to make sure they all went home in one piece. Even if she didn't.

Keir's face was screwed up in consternation, his hands clawing at the dirt as he was made to sit in what was surely an uncomfortable position. If he were to move no more than a millimeter in either direction, his throat would be sliced, right over his jugular. Antoinette didn't know what that meant for a witch whose life had been prolonged by magic, but she had a feeling, based on the look on his face, that whatever happened, wouldn't be good.

Khaos made to take a step forward, but Antoinette shot out an arm, blocking him from moving.

She narrowed her gaze, Jadis in her sight. "Let Keir go. I'll willingly go with you. You can take me to the Comte."

A low grumbling sound emanated from Jadis. All at once a screeching, demonic laugh burst past her lips. "He doesn't want you. He has me now. What he wants is the jewel. Give it to me, or tell me where it is, and all this ends. Simple."

Antoinette knew enough to know the Comte was only using Jadis as he had used her, for that's what he was, a user. He had no special skills of his own, no real intelligence. His charm was in his over-exuberant personality, which everyone who'd ever known him had tired of eventually. No one wanted him for long, and he didn't want them. Not once had they reached their expiration date. Antoinette had seemingly been the only exception to this. She believed the reason had been the novelty of who she was, Madame de Pompadour, the famous mistress.

Antoinette knew the only way to get Khaos's family to safety was to play a game with the Comte. "I don't have the jewel, but I know how to find it. Take me to him and I'll tell him what I discovered." Khaos sucked in a breath. She knew he was about to speak, so she held up a hand, and continued, "You can't kill all of us. Even if you manage to succeed in slitting Keir's throat, by the time you finish pulling the blade across his neck, Khaos and I will be on you. Can you handle us both? Even with magic? And if you manage to kill me, how will the Comte feel about that? He'll never find the jewel then."

Jadis laughed again. Keir winced as the blade was brought nearer his flesh. "I wonder, Antoinette. Have you asked yourself why *I* want the jewel?"

"What do you mean?" Antoinette unclenched her hands and wiped her damp palms on the sides of her jeans. There was something in the question that made her nervous. "You want the jewel to give to the Comte. I thought we'd already established that."

"Is that what you thought?" Jadis cocked her head to the side, a devilish grin on her face. "I care less about the Comte and more about what he wants to do to you. I'm going to help him with the spell to make you mortal, then I plan on taking your life myself."

Antoinette's brow creased, her frown deepening. "Why? I'm no one to you. Why should my demise matter so much?"

Jadis shook her head, her eyes rolling skyward. "I thought you were smarter than this, Antoinette. The Comte raves about how intelligent you are, how you advised a king, practically ran his court, and on and on and on. You haven't figured it out?"

Antoinette glanced up at Khaos, a question in her eyes. He shrugged, as confused as she was.

Jadis crouched down, digging her knee into Keir's upper back. He winced again, and she smiled that devilish smile. "I guess I'll have to spell it out for you. Those other witches, why did they come here?"

Realization slowly dawned on Antoinette. She took a deep breath, then said, "They came looking for a descendant of the witch who created the opal for me."

Antoinette thought back to that night in the Quarter. The night she'd sought out the powerful French Quarter witch. She had the same dark eyes, crinkled by age around the corners, and the same white hair.

"Don't you even remember her name?"

"I do. It was Maeve, and she looked an awful lot like you, especially around the eyes."

"Well, it took you long enough, Antoinette. Maeve was my mother, and you killed her."

Antoinette shook her head. "I didn't. I went to Maeve's house on Burgundy to collect the jewel. She handed it to me, I paid her, and I left. I did not hurt her."

Pain and anger contorted Jadis's face. "Not directly, no. But the spell she used to create the opal made her sick. She weakened in the days after. One evening, less than a week after she gave you the jewel, she laid down to rest and never woke. I was eight, Madame, eight years old when my mother died, leaving me an orphan with no way to fend for myself. Living on the streets as a female child is not easy."

Khaos put up a hand. "We're sorry for your lot, truly, but how can you know that your mother died as a result of the spell? She could have died from any number of things."

"My mother was a powerful witch," Jadis spat out her words. "She'd thrived for three hundred years. The only thing capable of taking her down was a spell powerful enough to drain her of her power." Jadis pressed her knife further into Keir's flesh, a sneer on her face. He gasped.

"Stop." Antoinette held up her hands. "I'll go with you. Gladly. Just please let them go, let them all go. If you can produce Fosette and Lucian and let these four people leave peacefully, then I'll go without a fight."

Khaos growled next to her. "Over my dead body," he said.

Antoinette couldn't look at him. If she did, she may have lost her resolve. Instead, she kept her focus on Jadis and Keir. "This isn't your choice to make. It's mine. I've already put too many innocent people in danger. I'm going. End of story. Take Keir and his parents and get them clear of this place."

"That sounded like an order." Although his voice was gruff as always, there was a softness around the edges. Antoinette knew that no matter what had happened between them, leaving her here would be nearly impossible for him.

She adopted a softer tone, looking up into his eyes as she used her old trick and dug her fingernails into the palm of her hand to keep from crying. "Please, Khaos. Please do this for me. Keir and his family are innocent in this. Take them away from here. I can handle the Comte." Looking Khaos in the eye was even harder than Antoinette had anticipated. As she gazed at him, she realized something. This man could take away her pain, erase her loneliness in one fell swoop. But she also realized something else, he never would. No one would. Antoinette had only herself.

Khaos set his jaw, his eyes as cold as steel. "Fine, but once I have them to safety, I'm coming after you."

Antoinette had never had anyone fight for her before. She didn't know how to use her words to respond. All she knew was that her knees had suddenly gone weak and the burning in her throat had intensified. She pressed her nails harder into her flesh, feeling the blood seeping out. All she could do was nod and blink away the tears.

She then returned her attention to Jadis. "Release him and bring the others out. There won't be a fight."

"Not at the moment," Khaos said under his breath.

Antoinette almost laughed but didn't. She should have known better. He just couldn't help himself.

"Deal." Jadis removed the knife from Keir's throat, then kicked him forward with the tip of her boot. Keir splayed out in the dirt, sucking down mouthfuls of air. Khaos leaned down, grabbing Keir under the armpits and hauling him to his feet.

Antoinette moved alongside Jadis, her hands down at her sides, unclenched to seem non-threatening.

Jadis held her knife half out, just in case one of her enemies decided to get rowdy. "Lucian is inside, you two can get him after we leave."

Antoinette's stomach sank like a stone. "And Fosette? Where is she?"

Jadis shrugged. "Fosette is with the Comte. I'm sure he'll release her once he has you."

"That wasn't the deal." Keir was still huffing breaths as he stood, half bent over next to Khaos. "You said my mother was here."

"I agreed," Jadis spat out, "that I would let you all go if Antoinette came with me. I have to get to Fosette to do that, as she isn't here."

"You could have told us she wasn't here." Keir regained some of his breath, standing a little taller. "You're manipulating us."

"You're the one who assumed she was here." Jadis backed up a few steps. "Now, we have places to be."

Before Antoinette knew what was happening, Jadis had sheathed her knife, pulled a small bag from her shirt pocket, and thrown the bag on the ground. She took hold of Antoinette's arm as a hail of white dust exploded around them. Antoinette heard someone yell, presumably Khaos, but within seconds everything was quiet. She'd closed her eyes against the assault of powder. When she opened them, she was no longer in the clearing, she was in a courtyard.

CHAPTER SIXTEEN

Khaos lunged forward, grabbing Antoinette through the dust, but half a second before he reached her, she was gone. She'd disappeared like a rabbit in a magic act.

"Gods dammit," he yelled, spinning around to make sure Antoinette was really and truly gone. There was an ache in his chest, a pain behind his eyes, and for some reason the back of his throat burned. He'd lost her, and this time she hadn't slammed the door on his heart, she disappeared into thin air with a witch who wanted her dead.

Behind him, he heard scrambling in the dirt and looked back to see Keir sprinting toward the cabin. As much as Khaos hated to admit it, the first order of business was to get Lucian and take them back to New Orleans. From there, he'd have to devise a plan on how to find Antoinette and Fosette, quickly. He knew he wouldn't have much time.

He tried to put Antoinette from his mind and followed Keir to the cabin.

Lying in the middle of the dusty floor was Lucian, bound and gagged, and unconscious. Keir knelt, pressing his fingers into the side of Lucian's neck. Fear wound through Khaos's belly like molten lava until he saw Lucian's chest move up and then down. At least he was alive.

Keir leaned over Lucian, gathering him in his arms. Khaos followed suit, slipping the gag from Lucian's mouth so he could breathe easier, then made quick work of untying the cord that held his arms behind his back.

"Dad," Keir said as he shook Lucian. "Dad, wake up. Can you hear me?"

Lucian groaned, his eyes squeezing shut before fluttering open. "Where's your mother?" Lucian tried to get up, but Keir held him in place.

"Get your bearings before you try to get up."

Lucian ignored him, pushing Keir to the side so that he could stand. "Where is your mother?" he asked again as his gaze cast about the interior of the small cabin, looking past Khaos as if he didn't see him.

"She isn't here, Dad." Keir stood, also looking around the one-room cabin. "The witch took her and Antoinette to wherever this Comte is."

Lucian went to the table, rifling through the empty jars that littered the top.

"Dad, what are you doing?" Keir swiped a hand through his thick brown hair. "I told you she's not here."

Lucian stopped long enough to send a pointed look toward his son, and then Khaos. "The two of you have never been in a position where you've had to find someone, and that's never been more obvious. I'm looking for clues. Haven't you ever been in an escape room? Look around. The witch would have left some kind of information behind. Clearly, she resides here at least some of the time."

Lucian was right. The cabin, though dusty, was lived-in. The cot in the corner was covered by a handmade quilt that looked clean. There was a wash basin near the cot that was half filled with water, and left on the stove were the remnants of an egg and toast breakfast. The witch wasn't tidy, but she did live in the cabin, at least from time to time.

Khaos went to the bed and pulled back the quilt. There was nothing there but white sheets and a pillow. He went to the chest at the end of the bed and flipped open the lid. If they could find an indication as to where the Comte was, he could get to Antoinette and Fosette faster.

The chest was crammed with liquid-filled bottles and plastic bags full of powder and herbs. "Her magical accoutrements," he said.

Lucian trotted over and nearly shoved him to the side. Khaos was twice his size, but his uncle was running on adrenaline. "Did you see the witch take Fosette?" he said, running a hand over the contents of the chest.

Keir shook his head. "No, she was gone when we arrived, but we saw her take Antoinette."

Lucian sat back on his heels. "This is good. That means that the method she used to move Fosette was likely the same one she used to take Antoinette. Tell me what you saw. Did she use a crystal, a liquid, a powder?"

"It was a powder," Khaos said. "I tried to reach out for Antoinette, but only felt dust."

"Color?" Lucian asked. "If I can engineer the powder, it might be able to take us to the same location."

"Of the powder? White, with some light blue mixed in." Khaos looked down at his arm. There was a residue on the sleeve of his leather jacket. He held his arm out to Lucian. "Does this help?"

Lucian grabbed his arm. "Good boy," he said.

Khaos made a face, but as Lucian was still on the ground, he didn't see it.

"Khaos, don't move." Lucian dug his hands into the chest, jostling the contents. He drew out a mortar and pestle, stood, and went to the table at the far side of the room. Setting these down, he pulled out the pestle and set it aside. He then tore off a piece of his shirt near the bottom and went back to where Khaos stood with his arm stuck out in front of him. Lucian then wiped off the residue with the piece of fabric.

Back at the table, he dropped the residue-soaked fabric into the bowl. He cupped his hands over the mortar and recited several words that Khaos couldn't understand.

Smoke rose from the pestle and filled Lucian's hands. Lucian recited several more words and the smoke cleared. He looked at Keir, then at Lucian with a smirk. "I can recreate this potion and the spell that went with it."

Relief flooded Khaos's senses. "What does that mean? You can take us straight to them?"

"Yes. I only need a few minutes and we'll be on our way."

Keir stepped forward. "Should we get help first? Desiree, Jaxon, and Theron would be able to get here quickly."

Lucian shook his head. "There's no time. We have no idea what's happening to your mother and Antoinette. The sooner we act, the better."

"Agreed," Khaos chimed in, finally lowering his arm. The witch told us point-blank that she intends to kill Antoinette. I can't imagine Fosette will be much use to them, either. Besides, we have the element of surprise on our side. They won't be expecting us to have found them so quickly, certainly not in this way."

"The time to act is now," Lucian agreed. "We have two witches and a demon on our side."

"Dad," Kier interrupted. "She got the better of you and Mom."

"Exactly, Son, because she took us by surprise. Now it's our turn." Lucian took a deep breath. "Now, Son, take the piece of my shirt out of the mortar."

Keir did as he was told, then Lucian dropped the powder back into the bowl. "Here we go, boys."

Khaos squared his shoulders, readying for a battle he knew was about to come.

CHAPTER SEVENTEEN

The courtyard where Antoinette now found herself was familiar to her, as all French Quarter courtyards were.

The bricks underfoot were uneven and mossy; the walls surrounding her were slathered in a plaster coating, deep cracks forming after centuries of holding form. The sky above her was dark, but brilliant with stars. Gas lamps flanking a dark doorway cast a soft flickering light. The scene should have been a charming and romantic one, but she knew very well that it was not. This scene was a façade, the loveliness hiding the monstrousness within.

Jadis was behind her, pushing Antoinette forward, the palm of her hand thrusting into the middle of her back. "Move," she hissed.

Antoinette didn't need instructions to know that the Comte waited for them inside. She closed her eyes for a beat, taking a deep breath into her lungs. There was only one way through this mess. That way was forward: forward toward the Comte, forward to the opal, and forward to Fosette.

Antoinette put one foot in front of the other.

One step at a time.

She said this repeatedly as she walked through the

courtyard doors and into a sumptuously decorated sitting room. She hadn't expected anything less. The Comte couldn't stand mediocrity. Only the finest would do for his taste. He believed himself more worthy than a king.

Antoinette thought she had steeled herself, but in reality, nothing could have prepared her for facing him. She hadn't seen him in over a hundred years. So long, more than a lifetime. The years had felt like an eternity.

She took a deep, steadying breath, then took in the room. A figure loomed by the fireplace. There he was, his back to her, an elbow resting on the mantle as he stared down into the flames.

The breath caught in the back of her throat. She would have known him anywhere, even after so long. His hair was still the warmest shade of brown, his back straight and proud even as he bent his neck downward. His left hand was loose, hanging by his side, rather small and delicate for a man, just as she remembered. The Comte wasn't small. He was tall and relatively fit, but his hands always took her by surprise, as they were only slightly larger than her own.

"Here you are, Antoinette, after all this time." He spoke into the flames, not bothering to turn around. She knew he was doing this for dramatic effect. The Comte was all about effect. He craved drama as much as he craved wealth and recognition.

"Here I am," she said. What else was there to say? She was here, his prisoner once more, but if she had anything to say about it, she wouldn't have to be in his presence any longer than necessary.

Slowly, the Comte turned to face her. His slow turn was almost comical, meant to give Antoinette time to take him all in. She nearly laughed but smothered her mirth with a small cough. Now was not the time to anger him. If she wanted to get her hands on the jewel, she would have to play his game, especially with the witch watching her every move. The witch who wanted her dead for a crime that wasn't hers.

It wasn't until the Comte had turned toward Antoinette and looked her in the eye that her plan started to come together. Her original thought had been to fight her way out. Perhaps Fosette was strong enough to help, and combined, they could both escape. But with Fosette nowhere in sight, indeed, and the powerful Jadis staring her down, Antoinette was going to have to adjust.

She wiped the concern from her brow, allowing a small smile to quirk up the corners of her lips. "You're more handsome than I remembered," she breathed.

Two things were imperative to her plan. The first was to shamelessly compliment the Comte, and the second was to deliver her compliments in a way that would remind him of her shyness. The Comte loved a shy woman, a woman who wanted him but was also afraid of the wanting. She'd resisted him mightily when she'd been his captive. Now, she must convince him she'd wanted him all along but had been afraid of her feelings. Antoinette was used to complicated machinations. She'd perfected them at court, where she often had to make people feel a hundred different ways in a single day to survive. She was an expert survivor. An expert thriver. Had she played the Comte's game all those years ago, perhaps she'd never have been his captive at all. But she'd been tired, weakened not only by her years at court but by the vampirism she hadn't wanted. She hadn't known how to make it work for her. No one had taught her how to use her preternatural strengths. Now she was ready to pull from every resource she had.

The Comte's face changed as soon as Antoinette delivered her first compliment. When he'd first turned around, he'd looked at her with a hint of disdain, one eyebrow raised as if beholding a disobedient child. But the second she spoke, the eyebrow fell, the eyes widened just a touch, and his chin tipped up ever so slightly. He was as prideful as a peacock.

"Thank you, my dear," he said, his voice simpering in a way that made her skin crawl. "You, too, are lovelier than I remember." He smiled at her, perfect white teeth gleaming like floodlights.

Antoinette pinched the back of her hand, and her smile came, forced but full.

Jadis sank into a chair, flinging one leg over an arm like a pirate in a movie. She scoffed. "This one is playing you. Don't fall for it."

Antoinette feigned shock, pressing a hand to her chest. She knew the angle to play here, and it had nothing to do with her. "That chair must be over a hundred years old, and the fabric is the finest silk. Please don't defile it in such a way." Antoinette couldn't have cared less about the chair, but she knew how much the Comte would fret over something so materialistic.

He tore his gaze from Antoinette to sneer at Jadis, sitting akimbo in his chair. "Yes, do please sit like a lady."

Jadis scowled at Antoinette but removed her leg from the arm of the chair. "Give us the opal so we can get this over with. It's time to end your sad existence and for me to be on my way." Jadis adjusted her seat but didn't rise.

The Comte cleared his throat, a sly smile playing on his lips. "Jadis, I hate to tell you this, but I've had the jewel all along. What I wanted was Antoinette."

Shock caused a momentary shutdown of Antoinette's senses, but she quickly recovered. Her face betrayed nothing. "You have the opal? How?"

Jadis sneered, shooting to her feet. "What are you talking about, you goofy old man? You've had me out searching for days. You promised me the opal for my revenge, and I'll have it."

The Comte silenced Jadis by raising his hand. He looked at Antoinette, smug satisfaction in his eyes. "I'm the one who stole your jewels from the police all those years ago. After I mesmerized the jailers, then the officer pivotal in my capture, taking them along with my Rembrandt was easy. With the help of another witch, I hid them with a spell which is how I found out about the opal."

The Comte wanted to impress Antoinette with these facts. She could tell by the look on his face.

Antoinette had to think and fast. Several important bits of information had been revealed. The Comte and Jadis were only partners in this one thing, and he'd played her, too. The Comte did love his games and manipulations, and it seemed as if he'd played Jadis for a fool. All he'd wanted was for her to do his dirty work, which was to bring Antoinette to him. And if the Comte had wanted her dead, all he'd had to do was give the opal to Jadis. No, he was playing more than one game here. This meant it would be easier for Antoinette to drive a wedge between them. No one played a better game than she did.

Antoinette affected her best pout, made even more delicious by her thick lower lip. She jutted her juicy lip, lowered her chin, and batted her lashes at the Comte. Antoinette knew to do this by only a degree, too much would be seen as artful. "Strange that you want to kill me after how close we were at one time. I don't even know what happened to you after that horrible night. Why have you never come to me as a friend?"

The Comte narrowed his eyes, his head cocking to the side, taking her measure with a slow gaze.

Jadis scoffed. "Don't fall for her lies and nonsense. We know that she had the opal made. She intended to kill you all along. She's the one who had your home raided that night. Nothing else makes sense."

The Comte held up a hand, cutting off further commentary from the witch.

Antoinette played at being aghast. "You think I was going to kill you with the opal? No." She shook her head. "The opal was for me all along. I was going to use it on myself. This was always my intention."

"She lies." Jadis moved forward a step. "Get the opal so I can kill her now. No more games."

"Don't forget *you* work for *me*." The Comte looked at Antoinette but spoke to the witch.

Antoinette knew he couldn't see past her façade. People had only ever seen what she wanted them to. "I didn't call for the police either. How could I have done that? I never left the house. If you follow the witch's logic, why would I do so if I planned to use the opal on you? And why would I do it if I planned to use the opal on myself, which I did? The police coming to the house would have been irrelevant to me, as I'd already decided to become mortal and die."

The Comte's hand remained raised as he studied Antoinette from head to toe. After a few seconds, Jadis nearly seething like a feral dog the whole time, the Comte spoke, "I think she might be telling the truth."

"What?" Jadis roared. Anger was coming off her in waves of heat.

Antoinette took a small step back.

"How can you be so fucking stupid? Or are you just thinking with your cock?" Jadis stared at the Comte, murder in her eyes.

The Comte's attention finally moved from Antoinette to Jadis.

Antoinette took the opportunity to look for clues to Fosette's location within the home. She remained calm and steady to reach out with her vampiric senses. Fosette was immortal, but she was human. All Antoinette had to do was listen for breathing outside of the sitting room.

She blocked out what was happening with the Comte and Jadis and focused on the sound of breath.

In seconds, she was rewarded for her patience. Someone was breathing softly, likely in sleep, beyond the double doors behind her. The doors didn't appear locked; even if they were, a lock could hardly keep her out.

Fosette was likely unconscious, meaning if Antoinette had to move her and fight her way out, the situation could prove difficult. Best to stoke the fires between the Comte and Jadis and use their tussle as a distraction.

"That language is not appreciated under my roof. I believe we've had this conversation before," the Comte said to her.

Jadis was standing, her fists clenched at her sides, a feral snarl marring her features. "I've had enough of your stupidity, you fop. I'll say whatever the fuck I want. Now, I'm going to get that opal from you. We're going to complete the ritual to make her human, and I'm going to take her pretty little head. Understood?"

Antoinette took a step back, then another one.

"No, I'm afraid the terms of our arrangement have changed. I'll pay you for bringing Antoinette to me, and then it's time you were on your way. I'm sure you have some filthy swamp home to return to."

"That's it, you fuck. I'll kill you both the old-fashioned way." Jadis let out an animalistic yell, throwing her hands out at the Comte. Blue light shot forward, which the Comte ducked.

After that, pandemonium broke out in the room. When the Comte launched himself at Jadis, Antoinette pivoted, turning one of the knobs to the French doors behind her. The room she found herself in was an office, all masculine colors and heavy furniture. And there, lying on a leather sofa, was Fosette, still dressed in the same dress she'd worn during Antoinette's visit.

There was yelling, shouting, and furniture breaking behind her. Through all this, Antoinette focused on Fosette. Although Fosette was a good seven inches taller than she was, Antoinette was still a vampire, with more than enough strength to carry someone five times her size. She scooped her arms under Fosette's body and flipped her over a shoulder.

There were doors leading to the courtyard from this room, so they wouldn't have to go back through the ruckus in the sitting room.

Antoinette kicked open the doors, heedless of the shattering of glass, then sprinted to the middle of the courtyard. She didn't want to slow down but needed a second to get her bearings, so she stopped near the fountain at the back, gazing up and around the high walls. She'd go for it and jump the wall. The fact that she was capable wasn't the question, the question was if she was capable of making such a jump carrying a human being in her arms. Antoinette had never had to test herself in such ways. Yes, she was a vampire with all the unnatural powers that came with being a vampire. The problem was, she'd never practiced, never tested her limits. She'd led a quiet life in the back office of Noir, never leaving to do much of anything.

The last few days were a wholly new way of life for her.

A few days? It feels like it's been a few years.

Antoinette adjusted Fosette in her arms, readying herself to leap onto the top of the courtyard wall. Just as she was about to leap, two things happened at once—the sounds of fighting ceased inside the townhouse, and Khaos and Lucian appeared right before her.

"Fosette," Lucian cried, pulling his wife out of Antoinette's arms, cradling her body to his as she hung limp.

"Is she alive?" Khaos choked on his words, hovering over his uncle.

"She's alive." Antoinette pointed to the open courtyard doors behind her. "But we need to leave now. The Comte and his witch are in there, and I expect one or both of them to emerge from that doorway any second."

Khaos offered Antoinette one glance before he turned his back on her. "This ends now," he said, barely more than a growl.

"Finally, we agree on something," Keir said as he stared down at his mother.

Antoinette reached out to grab the back of Khaos's jacket, but he was already five paces ahead of her. She glanced at Lucian, who had lain Fosette on the courtyard stones. He was fishing something out of his pocket, murmuring words Antoinette couldn't understand.

It wasn't the Comte who Antoinette was worried about. Khaos could end him with a swipe of his hand. She was worried about Jadis. Witches were dangerous, unpredictable creatures. Yes, Khaos was a demon, but could he hold his own against a witch like her? Could he fend off her spells? What about Keir? She knew nothing of his talents.

Antoinette felt the breath go from her. Her chest tightened, her stomach pinching. She knew what it meant. She was afraid for Khaos, afraid he would get hurt, or worse, killed. She couldn't allow that, she'd rather it be her, not because she was the cause of all this mess, but because if he were gone from the world, where would that leave her? She needed him here, in this world, with her. Maybe she wouldn't use the spell on herself, maybe, if Khaos would have her, she would spend an eternity with him. Maybe. That was a discussion for another time. At that moment, she would have stepped into a fire for him, so she did just that. She fortified herself and ran through the courtyard doors, into what was once a lovely little parlor, though there was nothing lovely about it now.

Someone could have told Antoinette that a tornado had swept through the place, and she would have believed them. The devastation was on another level. Shards of wood that had once been beautiful antique furniture now littered the ground, so much so that there weren't many places to step. The door she'd gone through to get to Fosette was loose, half hanging from a hinge.

Lying on his back in the middle of the rubble was the Comte. One hand lay on his chest as he gazed up at the ceiling, the other idly played with bits of broken wood. He looked like a man quite at his leisure, gazing up at the sky during a lazy afternoon. Other than the rumple of his once perfectly pressed clothes, he didn't appear to have been in a fight for his life.

Jadis, however, was nowhere in sight.

"Where is she?" Antoinette stood stock still, not trusting the situation for one second. Khaos turned to her, gripping her upper arm gently and pulling her back to stand next to him.

The Comte's hand, the one idly resting on his chest,

waved at the air. "I believe she went poof," he said.

"What do you mean she went poof?" Antoinette liked the feeling of Khaos's hand on her arm. He hadn't moved it. He continued to hold her in place next to him, and she liked it.

"I think he means she vanished as witches like to do." Khaos was staring down at the Comte, a confused expression on his face. "This is the Comte I've heard so much about?"

"It is."

Khaos made a noise in the back of his throat. "This man is what my father would call a dolt. He doesn't look like he's been useful to anyone a day in his life."

Antoinette eyed Khaos's profile. "He hasn't. He's been the very opposite of useful." She had to wonder what Khaos was thinking. Was the brat prince staring down at another brat prince realizing what a waste his life has been? Was he thinking that maybe he wanted to change all that? Antoinette longed to pull him aside and talk to him about this and a hundred other things, but this wasn't the time.

"What do we do with him?" Keir asked.

All this while, the Comte had remained in his lupine state, not eager to run or join the conversation. Antoinette almost felt for him at that moment. The fire had appeared to have gone out of the man.

"I think we leave him to himself. You and your family go back to your lives, and I prepare myself for Jadis. It's a guarantee that she'll be paying me another call."

"There are many things wrong with that statement." Khaos released her arm, crossing his and facing her. "Let's unpack them one by one."

Just as Antoinette was about to respond to Khaos, the air crackled near the mantle. Jadis stepped forward through white smoke, Antoinette's long-lost opal gripped in one hand. "The time for that call is now, Antoinette," she sneered.

CHAPTER EIGHTEEN

Antoinette's blood went cold at the sight of her opal clutched in Jadis's hand. She knew that all Jadis needed was a single drop of her blood to touch the face of the jewel, and then Antoinette would be mortal. After that, anything fatal to a human would kill her, too. Ending her as a vampire was more difficult. Antoinette had met vampires in the catacombs who'd survived immolation, beheading, and one who lived after meeting the sun. The only sure way she knew was to remove the head, thus rendering the creature immobile, burning the head and the body to ash, and scattering the dust to the four winds. Mortals were much easier to kill.

The murderous look in Jadis's eye only added to Antoinette's terror. She had something now that she wanted to hold on to—*someone* she wanted to hold on to. She was going to have to fight for her life.

Khaos tensed next to her, but Antoinette wasn't interested in Khaos fighting her battles. She'd asked enough of him and his family. Not only that but if something happened to him, she wasn't sure she could go on. No, this was her fight and her fight alone.

Surely, Jadis expected her to duck and cover, so

Antoinette did the unexpected. In the unexpected, there was surprise. If Antoinette knew anything, it was the benefit of taking people by surprise.

When Khaos tried to push Antoinette behind him, she pivoted, running straight for Jadis.

Khaos yelled behind her, but Antoinette didn't hear what he said, all of her focus was on the witch. For a split second, Jadis was caught off guard. Her eyes went wide as she flinched backward. For a moment in time, as Antoinette sped over debris, launching herself over the still-prone Comte, she thought she had her. Jadis was frozen in shock as Antoinette reached out a hand. And then, everything changed in an instant. Jadis dodged her arm, deflecting her to the side as she stepped away. Antoinette nearly lost her balance but rallied quickly, turning to face Jadis, but she was no longer there.

"Dammit, Antoinette," Khaos yelled from across the room.

Antionette turned to face him. There was a flash in the corner of her eye. It was a diversion. A hand, oddly strong, grabbed a fistful of her hair from behind, a sharp knee in her lower back sending her to the ground.

They were facing Khaos, who'd moved to rush forward but was now frozen in place, his wide, panicked eyes staring down at Antoinette as she knelt in front of him. Keir was still standing in the same spot, a look of bewilderment on his face.

"Stay where you are," Jadis screeched. "I deserve my revenge, and everyone here knows it."

A snarl contorted Khaos's face as he stared hellfire at Jadis. "You deserve nothing," he said. "No one is to blame for your mother's death. I will, however, be to blame for yours."

"We'll see about that." Jadis scratched Antoinette's cheek as she kicked her forward, into the rubble. "One drop is all it takes."

Khaos yelled, deep and guttural, as he rushed forward,

Antoinette pushing herself up from the ground.

Before Antoinette could register much, Fosette and Lucian ran into the room. Lucian threw a white powder on the ground. Fosette chanted words Antoinette couldn't understand.

The room spun, the landscape shifting out from under her. She knew what was happening. She was once again being transported somewhere new. Only this time, it wasn't Jadis in control, it was her friends.

When the room stopped spinning, and Antoinette was able to get her bearings, she felt a great rush of wind blow by her.

She looked up, still dizzy, to see Khaos rush Jadis, knocking the opal from her hand.

Antoinette gained her feet, but not before snatching the opal from the ground. Her blood hadn't touched the stone, and she breathed a sigh of relief.

Lucian pushed her aside, flinging his hands out. Cords of blue light flew from his palms, wrapping around Jadis until she was bound tight, kicking and straining to no avail. Her face was red, spittle sliding from the corners of her mouth. "How dare you? You have no right to bind me."

"We have every right," Lucian said, his hands falling to his sides. "We're going to make sure you can't hurt anyone ever again."

Jadis laughed like a maniac as she writhed in her bonds.

Antoinette looked around her for the first time. She was in a parlor with lovely silk furniture and beautiful seventeenth-century art on the walls. Keir was there, as were Fosette, Lucian, and, of course, Khaos. Almost comically, the Comte lay on the wood floor exactly as he had at the townhouse, unbothered by what went on around him.

Two women and a man, all strangers to her, stood off to the side, their faces a mixture of surprise and amusement. The women matched Fosette with their beauty. One had fiery red hair, wearing a sumptuous silk gown that Antoinette would have worn once upon a time. The other was dark-haired, pale-skinned, and equally pretty in a modern wrap dress.

The man had to be a demon like Khaos. There was no doubt they were of the same species, as their sheer size was wholly unnatural. The man's face, stormy and perplexed, addressed the room, "What the hell is going on here?"

"Oh, you know, Theron. We wouldn't be us if there wasn't some sort of drama." Fosette turned to face him. "We have much to tell you."

"Hold on, Mom." Keir stepped forward, one hand shoved in a pants pocket. "Let me give Uncle Theron the Cliff's Notes version."

Antoinette listened as Keir gave the rundown of what had transpired. When he introduced Antoinette to them, the woman named Desiree bustled over to her, her hand outstretched. "Imagine Greer," she said over her shoulder. "Would you ever have dreamed the famous Madame de Pompadour would be standing in our parlor?" Desiree shook Antoinette's hand warmly.

Greer came forward. "You are most welcome."

"Thank you." Antoinette took her hand. "But I'm so sorry to have brought this chaos into your home."

Greer smiled, bright and warm. "That's okay. We're used to a little chaos, aren't we love?" She looked toward her son with a twinkle in her eye.

Khaos laughed, dropping his head.

Theron remained on the fringe of the room. "Yes, this is all well and good, but what are we going to do with her"—he pointed at Jadis—"and him?" Theron pointed at the Comte, still in repose, staring up at the ceiling.

Fosette waved her hand. "We'll worry about him later. As to the witch, Lucian and I know exactly what to do. That's why we brought her here."

"What are you going to do with her?" Antoinette asked.

"Lucian, Keir, and I are going to open a transitive portal in the mirror there." She pointed to an ornate oval mirror hanging on the wall behind Jadis. "It's already a reflective portal. Lucian and I created it long ago so Greer could communicate with us and vice versa when she's in the Underworld. And when we're finished, you, my dear, will have the honor of kicking Jadis into literal Hell."

Jadis thrashed wildly, droplets of sweat flinging off her forehead. "You can't do this to me," she howled.

"She won't be able to leave?" Antoinette asked, ignoring the ravings of Jadis.

"No," Khaos answered. "No one except a select few ever leaves the Underworld."

Antoinette felt some guilt about this. Bound as she was, Jadis was hardly a threat, but they couldn't keep her bound forever.

"It's all right, Antoinette." Khaos must have sensed her uncertainty. He moved next to her, placing a soft, gentle hand on her back. "She'll never stop trying to hurt you. This is a mercy, as the woman has lost all sense and reason. She'll be calm in the Underworld, at peace. Not all of it is what you imagine. I'll tell you one day."

Antoinette tucked the opal in her pocket, her gaze on the red-faced Jadis. "Okay."

Fosette, Lucian, and Keir took hands forming a half circle in front of Antoinette and Jadis. As soon as they began chanting, Jadis went quiet, as if the fight had gone out of her.

The mirror bowed and seemed to go liquid, like something out of Wonderland. Fosette nodded to Antoinette, who went to take hold of Jadis.

Before Antoinette could get a grip on her, Jadis craned her neck to look Antoinette in the eye. "You'll see me again," she whispered with malevolence before kicking out a leg. Jadis pushed off from Lucian's chest, knocking him back a step, then dove headfirst, arms still bound at her sides, straight through the looking glass.

CHAPTER NINETEEN

The room was in a twitter, full of people, everyone talking simultaneously.

Antoinette would not be facing the witch again, not without him firmly by her side. Khaos had to make sure it was plain, in no uncertain terms, that she would never be alone again, not now, and not in the future. He'd realized something the second she was torn away from him back at the cabin—she was his priority, now and always.

"We have a few things to discuss." He tugged Antoinette off to a corner.

"The first issue I have with your previous statement is regarding that dirtbag." Khaos pointed to the side. "If you recall, you mentioned leaving him to himself. We're not doing that, not after—and I can't believe I'm about to say this—all the chaos he's caused. We either end him or use that opal of yours and make him human. Then, and only then, would I feel comfortable leaving him be."

Antoinette shook her head. "I need the opal for myself."

"No, you don't." Khaos looked deep into her eyes.

"Why not?" Antoinette tipped up her chin in a defiant gesture that almost made Khaos sweep her into his arms. "There's nothing left for me in this life. It's gone on long enough."

He placed a finger under that defiant chin. "There's nothing for you in this life, is there?"

Her eyes welled as she shook her head once to the left and once to the right.

"I'm here, Antoinette. As much as you may dislike me, as coarse and unrefined as you may find me, I only want you, now and forever." Khaos had never said anything so sappy. Not once in his long existence had he even thought to say such words, but now ... now he meant them with his entire soul.

Antoinette stilled under his touch. Her eyes went wide as she chewed on the inside of her lip, one he'd love to have a nibble on himself. "You want me?"

"Of course I want you, you silly woman. I thought I'd made it rather obvious over the last few days. How could I not want you? You're everything, Antoinette. I never thought I'd find you, and now that I have, I don't plan on letting you go." Khaos thought for a moment, then dropped his hand from Antoinette's chin. "Unless you don't want me? I know I'm a mess, but I plan on working on that."

Antoinette blinked, clearing the tears from her eyes. "I'm a mess, too. We can work on clearing up our messes together."

Khaos swiped an arm around Antoinette's waist, pulling her up until her face was right below his. "Together," he murmured, pressing his lips to hers.

Khaos had never in his life felt such soft lips. Antoinette's lips were like velvet. He quickly lost himself. The world fell away. He deepened the kiss, parting her lips with his tongue and diving inside her mouth. He fully intended on claiming her, on making her his.

Her hands slid over his chest, wound around his neck, and took hold of his hair. Khaos felt himself stiffen and knew if he didn't stop kissing her, he would have to claim her for all the world to see.

He pulled away, gazing into her languid eyes. "There's a

strange sensation in my belly. It's like a fluttering."

Antoinette giggled, a sound Khaos wanted to hear over and over until the day he ceased to exist. "Those are called butterflies. Have you never had butterflies before?"

"Never." Khaos chuckled. "I usually detest butterflies, too cute and delicate for my liking, but these butterflies I like."

"Please, don't let us disturb you." Desiree laughed her musical laugh.

Khaos glanced to the side to see the whole room staring. They were the focal point of everyone except Theron, who looked off into the distance like he'd rather be anywhere but there. Khaos couldn't help but grin at his mother, who smiled ear to ear.

Khaos set Antoinette back on her feet, then turned from her, begrudgingly, and faced the crowd. The Comte had moved. He now sat on the hard floor, pulling down his shirt sleeves. "I'll be off then, mon amis," he drawled. The Comte stood up in one elegant motion, then bowed.

"We're not your friends, and you're not going anywhere." Khaos would have to do everything in his power to keep from taking this little man's head off. Jadis might be gone, but the Comte was just as guilty.

The Comte looked down his nose at Khaos, then glanced at Antoinette. "This is the type of man you now spend your time with?"

"Yes." Antoinette took Khaos's hand. "And you better be careful—Khaos has quite the temper."

Khaos had to bite the inside of his lip to keep from smiling. He squeezed Antoinette's hand, doing everything he could to keep his focus on the Comte. The man may not look like a threat, but Khaos knew better than to underestimate anyone.

The Comte stuck one hand in his pants pocket, the other dangling in space. He looked like he was posing for a portrait, which made Khaos want to punch him even harder. "Fine. What is it you will have me do? Apologize?"

Now Khaos wanted to strangle him.

"Antoinette has decisions to make regarding the opal." Fosette folded her arms in front of her. "We'll turn our backs to give you a moment."

"That means you, too." Theron grabbed the Comte, spinning him by the shoulders.

With the modicum of privacy they'd been allowed, Antoinette raised her eyes to meet Khaos' gaze. He'd truly never seen such a beautiful face in all his existence, but her beauty was far more than her physical appearance. A light shone through her eyes that emanated from deep within. She was the definition of beautiful inside and out.

"What do you want to do, Antoinette? Truly?" Khaos still held her hand in his, and as far as he was concerned, he never wanted to let her go.

CHAPTER TWENTY

Antoinette felt a warmth deep in her soul. Gazing at Khaos, she saw a possibility she'd never seen before. Someone to love her fiercely and unconditionally. Someone who would never ask her to pretend to be something she wasn't.

"I'll tell you what I want," she started. "I want a man who loves me for what I am, not for what he would make me. The one great relationship of my life, my relationship with the king, was never about me, it was only about him. I cared for him, yes. He was a good man and a good king, but his love for me was based on what I could provide, not only in the bedroom but also socially, in the salons of Paris, and politically, as an advisor. He tired of me in the bedroom and was close to tiring of me elsewhere. I want someone who will love me forever, with no conditions attached. I want to be more than a mistress, I want to be myself. The Comte only wanted me for an ornament. I'm my own person and want to be respected, and I think you're the person for the job."

"I am," Khaos said, sweeping her into a fierce embrace.

He pressed his mouth to hers, possessing her with a single kiss in a way no one ever had before. This was a kiss full of future promises. Antoinette wanted more and more. For the first time in more years than she could count, she was excited for the future.

Even then, Antoinette could tell Khaos was holding back. This wasn't the place or time for the fullness of what they felt for each other. That time would come later, once they had dealt with the problems at hand and had each other well and truly alone.

She broke the kiss, her hand on the side of his face. "There will be so much more to say and do later." She smiled slyly. She could feel his body heat as he held her, a low growl emanating from deep within.

"Until later," he said against her lips, his breath hot and sweet.

Antoinette's knees went a bit weak, but she held it together. They had to press on with the tasks at hand.

She released him, and called out, "All right, I've made my decision."

When she had the attention of the room, the Comte standing with his arms crossed like a pissed-off teenager, Antoinette spoke. She knew what she wanted to do. The two-part plan had sprung, fully realized, to her mind. She wasn't sure if any of it would work, but for her, it felt important to try.

"I know what I want to do, but can he be unconscious?" Antoinette asked Fosette and Lucian.

"Easily." Theron, moving like lightning, snapped the Comte's neck. Instantly, the Comte fell into a pile of limbs at his feet.

"Great," Antoinette said. "I don't want to kill him."

Lucian had a wary look in his eye as he stood close to his wife, a hand on the small of her back. Fosette had a more resolute look on her face, her hands clasped in front of her.

Khaos bristled, a grunt issuing from the back of his throat.

"I don't. On his own, he's more of a pesky mosquito than a bloodthirsty lion. What I would like to do is use the opal to take away his immortality. We leave him whole and human. He really won't be a threat then. Unless there's someone else here who would like to use the magic on themself."

All eyes shifted toward Desiree.

Desiree shook her head, a bright smile on her face. "I've made peace with what I am. Besides, I couldn't do that to Jaxon. He needs me as much as I need him."

Antoinette wasn't sure who Jaxon was, but Greer slipped an arm around Desiree's shoulders, pulling her close.

"So, you've decided not to use it on yourself?" Fosette asked, one eyebrow raised.

"Yes." Antoinette glanced up at Khaos. "I have other plans for myself now. We'll make the Comte human and send him on his way. I'm fairly sure after that, he won't bother us again."

"Okay." Khaos massaged his chin. "Dad, grab a drop of that idiot's blood, and let's get this over with."

It only took a few drops of Antoinette's blood to awaken the Comte. Once he was seated, held fast around the neck by Theron, Fosette took the blood-soaked handkerchief and handed it to Lucian. While unconscious, Theron had sliced into the Comte's hand with Lucian's blade.

The Comte now sat, hugging his bleeding hand to his chest, a scowl marring his face.

Fosette took his undamaged hand in hers, placing the opal in his palm. The Comte tried to toss the gem, but Theron leaned down to hold his wrist with an iron grip. Lucian took the bloody rag and wrung it over the shining jewel. The opal sparked, a thin line of yellow haze emerging from the milky white. Instead of dissipating in the air, the haze traveled downward, enveloping the Comte's wrist, right below where Theron held him. The Comte seized once, then twice as the haze could be seen traveling through his veins.

In less than five minutes, the Comte was human, yelling epithets at them as he scrambled out the door.

Theron was the first to leave the parlor, but before doing so, he bowed low toward Antoinette. "I look forward to getting to know you," he said, then to his son, "Khaos … good job."

Keir gave Antoinette a quick hug, then stood by the door awaiting his parents, who both embraced Antoinette warmly.

"I can't thank you enough," Antoinette said to them.

"That's what family is for," Fosette said with a wink, then the three of them took their leave.

Antoinette thought her heart, full of joy as it was, might burst.

Greer and Desiree rushed forward, each taking one of Antoinette's hands. "We're going to be such wonderful friends, aren't we, Greer?" Desiree beamed at them.

"Of course. I knew this would be so when I first spotted Antoinette," Greer said, a sly smile on her face.

"What do you mean?" Antoinette asked.

"Yes, Mother, what do you mean?"

"Well, I told you I wanted you to meet someone, and that someone was Antoinette. I spotted her several weeks ago at a bar called Noir. Desiree was hunting a man who had committed a local murder, and while she was busy, I saw an unmistakable face. Madame de Pompadour herself came out to sign for a delivery. She disappeared quickly, but I knew who she was and what she was as soon as I saw her. I was only in your presence for a total of three minutes, Antoinette, but that was all I needed to know you were special."

Desiree grunted. "I can't believe you didn't tell me. Greer and her secrets," she said to no one, then laughed.

"I just had a feeling you would be important to us." Greer hugged Antoinette. "And now I think it's time you two were left alone." She smiled, pulling Desiree behind her.

EPILOGUE

Khaos had never awakened next to a woman without wanting to bolt, but he did that evening. Contentment was a wonderful feeling.

He stretched his legs in the dark, his feet dangling off the end of her bed. One thing was for sure, she was going to need a bigger bed. He felt like he was hanging onto the side for dear life, especially since she was a bed hog, pressed up against him with at least three feet of space on her side. But he couldn't complain. He'd sleep on a balance beam if it meant he got to find himself in her bed each night.

They were happily ensconced in the little apartment over Noir. Khaos was manning the door each night while Deena stared at him wide-eyed. She still couldn't quite understand what Antoinette saw in him, but he was winning her over, bit by bit.

The woman from the dingy motel and her little boy, Henry, were now a part of the family. The woman, Marie, was working behind the bar, making ten times what she made in that awful motel room, Henry babysat by Mark, the former bouncer, and his daughter. Khaos and Antoinette had made good on their promises.

He and Antoinette had also gathered the rest of her jewels from the Comte. He'd dismantled a few, selling the stones over the years to fund his extravagant life, but many were still intact. They had long discussions into the night about what to do with them.

Antoinette stirred, her hair a tangle over his chest. Khaos kissed the top of her head. Content. Happy. Peaceful. This was all he ever wanted to be.

Enter the world of The Casket Girls, where forbidden love is the best kind.

In the shadows of 1728 New Orleans, a sinister fate looms over the casket girls, their lives hanging by a thread. A demon, condemned to an eternity as a bloodthirsty vampire, and a young woman stolen from her tranquil Parisian existence find their destinies intertwined. Together, they embark on a harrowing journey to liberate the casket girls from a fate more horrifying than death itself.

Available Now!

DON'T MISS ANOTHER FABULOUS SUPERNATURAL SERIES BY AD BRAZEAU- AVAILABLE NOW IN EBOOK AND PRINT!

Deepest Midnight

True love never dies.

For Millicent, a once French noblewoman turned immortal vampire, forever is a long time to live in despair. The love of her life is murdered the night she becomes immortal. Over two hundred years later, she locks eyes with an English actor, who happens to look exactly like her long dead love.

Sadness turns to happiness as Millicent and Jack find passion in each other's arms. Their fling quickly turns serious as Millicent finds joy once again—and possibly her one true love.

Their relationship becomes complicated by her own uncertainty and Jack's mortality. The other man in Millicent's life, her sire, Alexandre, isn't making the situation any easier. When Alexandre puts his foot down, Millicent must decide if she's going to continue to be led by others or take the reins and drive the outcome of her life.

Deepest Midnight is set in modern-day Savannah, Ga with occasional glimpses back to 18th century France. This is the first book in The Immortal Kindred Series.

EXCERPT

I reach into my clutch to take out my phone. Someone may as well get lucky tonight. Before I can begin my text, Alexandre is next to me. Being psychically linked to him stinks sometimes. Ok, all the time. If I wasn't so lazy, I would learn how to shield my thoughts.

I put my phone away. He says, "You know I hate texting."

"Why are you whispering? Who could possibly hear us?" I ask, in my sweetest southern belle accent. Irritating him is what I do best, although he doesn't always take the bait.

"Do you see her?" He pauses, looking around. "There she is in the back, next to the man with the copper hair. Don't you have a thing for gingers, Mills?" He tugs on my arm, pointing with his other hand, as I look up.

Alexandre starts explaining how he is going to approach her. I roll my eyes. He thinks he can just walk up to a world-famous movie star, throw up an eyebrow, and she'll be stripping naked. The annoying thing is, she probably will. On the last half of my eye roll, I lock eyes with a man who was murdered over two hundred years ago. All the breath leaves my body.

Rebel Heart

Always and Forever

Annie is a Culper Spy captured by Hessian soldiers. Powerful and mysterious Captain Thayer Emmerich takes mercy and releases her. Annie is inexplicably drawn to the handsome German, but she hates the feeling of powerlessness the enemy has left her with. Annie would give anything to be stronger.

One evening at the famous Green Dragon Tavern, Annie befriends the ethereal Millicent. Soon after meeting Millicent, Annie discovers her secret--her new friend isn't human. Millicent introduces Annie to her maker, Alexandre, and Annie joins their preternatural family.

Annie finally has the strength and freedom she needs to aid the revolution and see Thayer, once again. The two discover a passion neither has known before. But, too many complications exist for the pair to find happily ever after. Not only are they fighting on opposite sides of the war, the evil Emilia Romanov has plans for Thayer that do not include a love affair.

Rebel Heart is set in 18th century Boston and Savannah, as well as modern day Germany and France. This is the second book in The Immortal Kindred Series.

EXCERPT

Captain Emmerich took one brisk look to each side, then walked with an air of confident command toward the edge of the camp. It was dark with only a few lanterns lit and very few people about. This helped ease my anxiety. I tried walking with the same confidence, which was more difficult with my head down. The absurd cap threatened to fall off any minute, which would send a cascade of auburn curls falling around my shoulders.

Just as we were nearing the tree line, and I was beginning to relax, a soldier came running around the corner of a tent, right into the captain. The soldier snapped to attention, saluting. Captain Emmerich did the same, saying something in German. The young man relaxed, moving away.

As he walked by me, he looked me dead in the face, stopping in his tracks. I immediately put my head back down, but it was too late. It was obvious I was a woman in a man's uniform. There was no hiding this fact. The young man looked back at Captain Emmerich, turning as if he was about to run. The captain grabbed him by the neck with one hand. A sickening crunch reached my ears, right before the man crumpled into the mud.

"That was unfortunate," was all he said. The coldness of his voice shook me more than what he had just done.

I tried to hide my shock but knew I wasn't succeeding. "Why are you doing this for me? To kill your own man, it doesn't make sense," I said, still staring down at the young soldier.

"I'm beginning to wonder," he said as he grabbed my arm, yanking me into the dark woods. The trees looked ominous, and I hesitated just for a moment. Captain Emmerich took a handful of my uniform, at my shoulder this time, hauling me stumbling alongside him.

The King of Kings

Love has no limits...

Alexandre has retreated from the world. He has no one to love, nowhere to call home. While licking his wounds in the middle of nowhere, Alexandre is approached by Irish lass, Bria. She has a proposal for him; to follow her to Ireland and fight demons.

Alexandre finds this amusing, but intriguing. More than anything, he is curious to see the individual who sent Bria, someone from his ancient past.

In Ireland, Alexandre confronts a dilemma greater than fighting demons. He must face down fiends of all kinds, deciding once and for all who he really is. Sparks fly between Bria and Alexandre, adding to the already complicated situation. Can a bad boy vampire really change?

The King of Kings is set in southern Ireland with a glimpse back to Ancient Egypt.

EXCERPT

The finely decorated lobby was full of posh men and women, all wearing their best designer clothes and bespoke suits. Bria wasn't fazed in the least by her surroundings as she devoured a granola bar, crumbs falling to the marble floor. She was wildly out of place here and I kind of loved it. Her flaming hair was enough to draw attention. Her clothing, which screamed survivalist, made her that much more conspicuous.

I moved up behind her. "You deserve a spanking for the ruckus in the hallway."

"The man who spanks me is suicidal," she said in a loud voice, drawing even more looks from the guests and staff. Bria began walking toward the glittering revolving door, not bothering to see if I followed.

We took the train to the coast, making it just in time. Bria chided me the entire way for "sleeping in". I couldn't wait until we were on the boat with what I hoped was a roaring motor.

Goddess of the Moon

An impossible attraction. An apocalyptic threat.

After vanquishing a Celtic death demon, Selene should be kicking back and enjoying some free time. However, her life is anything but relaxed. She must travel to Romania, the last place she'd ever thought she'd be, facing another demon threat. Just another day at the office for the daughter of Cleopatra.

The situation soon escalates. The simple problem Selene thought she was facing, becomes intense--FAST. The dilemma is much greater than she initially feared. Throw in a sexy witch she doesn't want to be attracted to, and her life really gets complicated.

Overconfidence leads Selene to make a mistake which could cost everything. Can she unravel the mystery before it's too late? Or will her latest nemesis be the death of her and those she loves?

Goddess of the Moon *is the fourth book of The Immortal Kindred Series and is set primarily in Brasov, Romania.*

EXCERPT

Before I could pick up the first trunk, I heard it. The dull sound of cloven feet pawing at the soft grass. Not a tone a mortal could hear, but for me, the scraping was as clear as a bell. The sound barely preceded the smell. Demons typically had some sort of pungent, unpleasant odor. This guy was no different. He smelled of days' old refuse rotting in the sun.

I scrunched up my nose, releasing my tote which contained my laptop, letting it fall without grace to the earth. It was a good thing I paid extra for the durable case. If I was reading the situation correctly, the creature had me in its sights and would charge at any moment.

I knew what it was before I saw it, but this was not one of the creatures I had been hired to vanquish. The martolea were deceptive shapeshifters who could change their form at will. This one chose the form of a medium-size hound, as they most often did. Their diminutive size would lead one to believe they couldn't possibly be much of a threat. But, as with a vicious dog, these guys were deadly and strong.

Dark Star

The compelling final story in the enchanting series which began with Deepest Midnight....

The Immortal Kindred gather together as chaos erupts. Two of their own have gone missing, sucked back in time. Vampire demigod Selene messed with the wrong goddess of death. Now they're all in danger.

Millicent and Annie come face to face with the distant past. No longer immortal, they must draw on their inner strength to see them through travails long thought dead and buried.

Tash, the witch, draws on every spell he knows to bring the women home as he taps into the power of the dark star. Will it be enough to grant the immortals their happily ever after? Will the goddess, Nephthys, put an end to everything they know and love?

Dark Star is an epic adventure that will take you all over the globe and through time itself.

EXCERPT

After losing track of how far I'd gone, the path gave way to a clearing. At the center of the clearing was the cabin, as it was the night I came here in desperation. The assault on my senses was profound. It was like moving from one moment of déjà vu to another. I closed my eyes, my feet swaying a bit underneath me.

The small, rounded door swung wide. There he was. My breath all but stopped. Alexandre, dressed as a peasant in a loose white tunic over beige pants, stood with one hand on the open door and the other stretched out toward me. Here he was, the Jupiter from my dreams who became my maker, my friend, my lover, and almost my killer.

I admit, I wanted to run to him, to allow him to take me in his arms as he did the night my world turned upside down. I knew he would hold me tight, keep away everything that scared me. But I resisted. This me knew better than to trust him so blindly.

AVAILABLE IN EBOOK AND PRINT WHERE BOOKS ARE SOLD

AD BRAZEAU

ABOUT THE AUTHOR

A.D. Brazeau is an award-winning author who writes what she loves. From dark and fantastical fairytale retellings to quirky romance, and everything in between, she loves nothing more than to immerse herself in new worlds. A.D. Brazeau is a book-obsessed wife, mother, and dog lover, who grew up surrounded by stories. Not much has changed. A.D. is from Colorado Springs, Co.

www.ingramcontent.com/pod-product-compliance
Lightning Source LLC
Chambersburg PA
CBHW020123180626
46812CB00006B/2708